Gradation

KC Decker

ISBN-13: 978-1-7329645-1-8

ISBN- 10: 1-7329645-1-3

Gradation

noun:
gra•da•tion / grey•dey•shen

Definitions:

Gradation- A gradual change.

Tattoo Gradation- A visual technique of gradually transitioning from one hue to another.

Individual Gradation- A gradual progression in opinion, perception, or attitude toward another. Or, perhaps, a gradual change in your intolerance towards another human being—who, if we are completely honest, is really just a cocky bastard anyway.

Chapter 1

Friends. Ride or die, right? Always have your back. Know all your dirty little secrets. Love the shiny parts of you, and embrace the crappy ones? Yeah, well, I don't know about all that nonsense because my friends are just a bunch of assholes.

Granted, we have *murdered* a few bottles of overpriced Prosecco, which has vaporized their brain-to-mouth filters, but still—total assholes. I've long ago lost my ability to fight back, not that I ever stood a chance against their gang mentality in the first place. So, now I just have to sit here and take it. Actually, screw that, I still have some fight in me yet.

"Listen, you judge-y…. know-it-alls. It's hard to date nowadays. Guys just want to exchange explicit texts and pretend to be single, and if they ever *do* decide to meet, they are only looking for a hook-up. Those are *shark-infested* waters out there, and you two know it," I say, as I point to the other two single people at the table.

"And you," I redirect my clumsy focus to Arden and all her curly blonde hair, "Did they even have dating apps when you and Brady got together?"

"Three years, Alabama. We've been together for three years, not three decades. Yes, there were dating apps."

"There were also speeding tickets. And evidently, off-site blowies to get out of those tickets," Miles snorts. Which is precisely the type of thing Miles typically infuses into our happy-hour conversations—or any conversation, really.

"Hey! I went to court over that ticket!" Arden defends herself as well as can be expected against Miles' sanctimonious nature.

"Miles' affinity for dating apps is unquestionable. He would die of blue-balls if Grindr and Hornet were not at his fingertips within a moment's notice," Ivy laughs. She's single too, so I don't know why she insists on giving everyone else such a hard time about dating. The last few winners she dated were ones for the record book. One was on the seven-year plan for his undergrad degree in nautical archaeology, and the other huffed Scotchguard for fun.

"If we could all just refocus for a moment, I believe Alabama still wants to defend her atrocious taste in men," Miles states as he holds up an empty wine bottle and winks at our cocktail waitress. She, of course, blushes and I'm sure, dampens her panties because that's how people with heartbeats respond to Miles. He takes full advantage of it too, and really works hard to hone his *skill*.

"Why should I have to defend my taste in guys? There is nothing wrong with what *I'm* looking for. The problem is with what *they* have to offer." After I say this, I look around, waiting for someone to argue. They all just stare at me for a second and then, as a unit of assholes, burst into laughter.

"Remind us, Alabama, what has been the issue with the last—say, five guys you dated?" Arden asks with her happily-not-single, judgmental mouth.

"There were various prob—"

"Wrong!" Miles barks, interrupting me before I can hardly open my mouth. "We all know the problem, you are just too stubborn to admit having one." Now our waitress is back with another bottle of Prosecco, and it surprises none of us when she fills Miles' glass first.

"I'm gonna lump Ivy in here too," Arden starts from her soapbox, "Both of you date hot guys, first and foremost. Neither of you looks for substance, and then when they lack it, you act all surprised."

"No, it's just that we can't see their substance from across the bar," I try, but it sounds weak—even to me.

Ivy tries harder but has about as much success as I did. "We don't actually *seek out* guys that want to have sex with a bunch of women while letting us believe we are the only one—that's just how it shakes out. Guys our age don't want to settle down. They want to screw anything with tits and a viable pulse while continuing to advance their careers unhindered."

"Wrong," Miles states with a self-righteous sting to the word.

"Ok then, Almighty Miles, what *is* the problem?" I ask.

"Your pickers are broken."

"Huh?" I give a sort of verbal pause while I try to decode what he just said.

"Yep. Neither one of you could identify a good guy if one walked over and sat on your lap. Your pickers are broken."

"Why don't you introduce us to some good guys then? I mean, if your picker is so pristine and all-knowing, why don't you set us up with someone?" Ivy challenges, and if it's possible for gentle, innocent, brown eyes to blaze with hellfire—hers do at this particular moment.

"Trust me, you don't want me to set you up with the single guys I know." Then he coughs into his hand and mumbles, "And-they-don't-want-to-be-set-up-with-you."

"Stop it, you work with straight guys," Ivy pushes before she takes a sip of her drink and glares Miles down with a squinty-eyed stare. She's too sweet to pull it off, though, and there is zero true animosity between them.

"I work with finance guys. Let's fish in a different pond, shall we?" Then he sits up straight, suddenly all business, and says cryptically, "I have an idea."

I jump in, "Can I pre-empt this by just saying, no? The last time you had an idea, we all ended up on a party bike in ninety-five-degree weather, pedaling our asses off and drinking gluten-free beer from a warm keg."

"Just so we're clear, are you still mad about the cardio, or the gluten-free beer?" he asks, then waves his hands like he is trying to erase the question. "You know what? Never mind. Do you agree that your friends know you better than anyone?" he asks the group as a whole.

Reluctantly, we all look around before slowly nodding our heads. This is how Miles works. He hypno-glamours everyone into agreeing with his master plan. Then before anyone can stop it, we are caught in his sticky web and dazzled by his hypnotically spinning eyes. I'm serious, he's a frickin' Jedi Master.

"Ok, hear me out. If a person's friends know them better than anyone, isn't it reasonable to assume they know what works for you and what doesn't?" He leads us to the edge of his plan, but doesn't elaborate.

"Miles, shit or get off the pot," Arden says with the blow of one perfect curl out of her eyes. She may be impatient to hear his bright idea because it doesn't apply to her, but I'm not. I have visions of speed dating with an earbud receiver in my ear and a cow prod at my back.

"Ivy…Alabama, from now on, your friends are going to be your pickers."

Chapter 2

After some initial staunch protests, Ivy and I get caught up in the negotiations because apparently, we still have standards when putting our lives in someone else's hands.

Arden and Miles are almost militant in their defined parameters, and it makes me want to find some sister-wives and forget about dating and men altogether.

After more drinks and some questionable baked brie with fig and olive tapenade, the details of Miles' master plan are in place. First, they will make dating profiles for myself and Ivy. Here is the rub with that, though, neither one of us can have any say or input whatsoever with our own profiles.

Second, our friends will be the ones communicating on our behalf and lining up the dates. So, in this friend-encrusted universe, the first contact Ivy and I will actually have with the guys will be on our first date. Any pertinent information regarding the guys will be handed out like a stingy allowance right before meeting them.

Next, any and all follow-up communication has to be promptly addressed—all texts returned, all calls answered, and all subsequent dates agreed to. As long as the group still thinks it's a good match, Ivy and I have no influence on the matter. Miles insists this is necessary to avoid culling viable options from the herd prematurely or without merit.

If, for some reason, my friends no longer find the mark—I mean the date, worthy…only *they* can decide to end it. Otherwise, Ivy and I have to keep playing along, even if we don't like the guy.

Now, if you are anything like me, you've probably already figured out a loophole, right? I mean, how hard is it to be such a ghastly date that all you see are the guy's ass and elbows as he runs away from you?

Turns out, Arden and Miles were a little surprised by my sudden acquiescence to the whole ridiculous thing. They immediately identified my loophole and promptly put a three-month clause in place. Three months! As long as the trifecta of friends deems it appropriate, I have to continue the charade for ninety days!

You know what that means, right? Sex. And because none of them have to offer up their vaginas—or in Miles' case, his penis, they can work behind the scenes like an impulsive Geppetto, drunk with power.

Back to the three-month clause, because I can throw a date better than anyone. I'd rather cry during the whole thing while talking about a non-existent fiancé that I'm still in love with, than sleep with someone I don't want to. Hell, I'd even mention wanting babies right away if it kept someone I'm not interested in from kissing me. Anyway, I digress, the punishment for throwing a date deemed "a good fit" by my friends, is having to date someone *well below my station,* as Miles puts it. And trust me, they will go out of their way to line up someone for the punishment round, if only to find amusement in my suffering.

Somehow, my friends got me to agree to this nonsense. How, you wonder? I can answer that with one word.

Prosecco.

Chapter 3

When you work in advertising as I do, you know better than anyone how important branding is, or more specifically, how that brand is presented. So, when your three best friends take the brand that is *you*, and present it to the world however they please, it can be distressing.

The fact that I don't even have the password to my own dating profile is an affront to basic human decency. However, Arden and Miles are on their way to my loft right now, so they can *debrief* me before my coffee date.

Currently, Ivy is sitting cross-legged on my bed while I apply lip gloss and try to dig deep for an ounce of desire to meet this mystery guy. They have all been pretty tight-lipped about the whole thing and Ivy, who should have been more understanding because she is in the same boat, was unmoved by my begging and threats of violence to gain my password.

I even wrote hers on a folded piece of paper and slid it over to her so she could do some quality control on her own profile. She didn't bite. Then I resorted to pulling the damn thing up and turning the laptop toward her. She was unaffected. She wouldn't even glance at her own locked-down profile.

It's possible she is having fun with this, which is the polar opposite of how I feel. However, if I were to concede one thing about the process and my involvement in *her* profile development, it's that we, her friends, know her really well and probably answered the questions better for her than she would have.

When Miles and Arden arrive, I have put next to no effort into getting ready and already view this date as a walk down the green mile.

None of which sits well with Miles, who rounds the wall behind my bed to the open space considered my closet.

Arden flops down on the bed next to Ivy. They are both ready for the show, which is preceded by Miles' sharp reprimand from behind the wall.

"**No, Ma'am!** I have put too much into this process for you to approach it like a limp tuna. Now get up, take off the sweatshirt, lose the ponytail, and go plug in your curling iron." When he emerges, it's with a skirt, knee-high boots, and a sweater that would have been perfect ten pounds ago. He eyes me with amusement, then points to the bathroom, "I suppose you need to go shave too, right?"

***

Once I'm put together to their satisfaction, and far too primped for a Saturday, mid-morning coffee date, I have gleaned that my intended is a Scorpio and that his name is Gavin. That's it. I'd get more information from a fortune cookie.

"Are you serious? How am I supposed to identify him when I get there?" I ask after spitting toothpaste into the sink. "He thinks I've seen his pictures. Plus, if I have been communicating with him for two weeks, I should really know more regarding what I'm about to step in, right?"

"Good point. I'll show you a picture," Miles says as he pulls his phone from his back pocket. What he holds up on the screen makes me gasp and then take off my jacket and throw it at him.

"Nope," I say dismissively, as I lean down to unzip my boot. Then I notice that Ivy and Arden have both suddenly sat bolt upright on the bed.

"Why not? He is perfect for you!" Arden demands, thoroughly offended. I scowl at her, surprised I would even need to explain my resistance. Our answer comes from Miles, who doubles over laughing.

"Nah, that's not him. I'm playing, but you *are* communicating with this guy as well, just in case you have any reservations about making a good impression on your real date. I'm serious, Alabama. You *can't* sabotage this. Do you understand?"

I'm so relieved that the photo isn't of my real date that I find I'm suddenly more compliant. "At least tell me what we know about each other. I can't go into the lion's den without some basic knowledge of the guy I've been communicating with for two weeks."

Arden pipes up from across the loft, "He knows you work in advertising, are spiritual but not religious, and despise mayonnaise. He owns his own business, is very artistic, and prefers introverts."

"He is also really sexy, but—" Miles hesitates, and I wait for the hangman's noose.

"He is not your usual type. I mean…*at all.*"

Chapter 4

Within a minute of stepping foot inside the café, a man approaches me and asks, "Alabama?" He has messy blond hair, moody blue eyes, and a tattoo on the side of his neck that immediately puts me off. I go for clean-cut, Wall Street types, and this guy is—not.

"Hi, Gavin," I say, and it sounds disappointed, even to me. He doesn't even shake my hand as etiquette demands but instead places his palm presumptuously on my lower back and directs me to an empty table by the window.

"What are you drinking, whiskey? Tequila?" he asks as he takes his jacket off and then leans forward, resting his forearms on the table. His *heavily tattooed* forearms. Did I say he's not the Wall Street type? What I meant was, he is on the complete other end of the spectrum. This guy beat-up Wall Street and then backed his motorcycle over it.

"Huh?" I ask. My dad would have a stroke if I brought a guy like this home to meet him. How could my friends have been so far off? This has to be a joke.

"I'm teasing. How do you like your coffee?" he modifies as he straightens his posture.

"Oh, right. Cream and sugar, please," I say as I pull my wallet out.

"Don't worry, I've got this. It's not like you ordered a quad or a Kyoto cold brew—those would really tip the scales," he says as he smiles and gets up to head over to the counter.

Why in God's name did I agree to this? I've been given a grueling forty-five-minute minimum as part of the rules. I'm still inside the first five minutes, and I already want to leave. He's nice, but that's it. He's too gritty for me. He is no one I would ever date without my meddling friends forcing me to.

When he slides back into the booth, I quietly thank him, then he sits back and eyes me as if he's daring me to take a sip of the coffee. I feel like we are in some sort of a standoff, and the silence crackles between us like staticky sheets.

"So, what do you do for work?" I ask while trying really hard to sound interested. My question bores even me, but I've got like, thirty-seven minutes to burn.

"I run a tattoo shop," he says with a sleepy, almost growly voice. When he speaks, I get a glimpse of something shiny in his mouth. I think…yeah, his tongue is pierced. I can picture my mom right now, clutching her pearls and looking to my dad for fainting stability. Oh, the horror. Just the suggestion of their daughter going so wildly astray would be preposterous to them.

I try to picture this guy kissing me, and all I can think about is the little ball sitting on his tongue. It taunts me the whole time he talks. It's almost imperceptible, but now that I know it's there, it's all I can focus on.

"Enough about my work, how about you? Didn't you say you just got promoted?" he asks conversationally. *Actually, no. My friends told you that.*

"Yeah, I did." I leave it at that because I have no idea how much he already knows, and I don't want to sound like I'm bragging if I repeat everything he's already heard. My answer sounds a bit dismissive, but I'm not really the gloating type.

"How did that come about?" he inquires before he takes a squinty-eyed sip of his hot coffee.

"I slept with my boss."

He chokes on his coffee, then regains his composure after a few stout coughs. "Wow, that's impressive," he is smiling like a hyena, so he either knows I'm joking, or he is legitimately impressed with my methods.

"*Actually*, I had to outperform all the other reps. I delivered the highest BDI—sorry, Brand Development Index, eight out of the last twelve months. Now I handle all the exclusivity agreements—How many tattoos do you have?"

"Too many to count."

"How many piercings?"

"Two."

After no further explanation about his piercings and roughly twenty more minutes of banal conversation, I circle back to my promotion. I said his eyes were blue and moody before, but now they look sharp and cold. His mood has shifted, and now that he isn't even smiling, he's even *less* my type. I can picture him smoking a cigarette and strumming a guitar in the back of some dive bar. Maybe it's the hard set of his jaw. Was he this smoldering and tense before?

"I didn't really sleep with my boss to get the promotion. You know that, right?" He gives a non-committal nod, so I continue, "I mean, he has grandkids—not that that's the only reason. I would never do that. Mixing with men like him is not really my style." I'm starting to wonder if my rambling is to burn time, or if I truly don't have one single coherent thought besides hitting the timer at forty-five minutes on the dot.

"Good for you. Now, can I be honest?" he asks, but it's really not a question. It's a prelude to something arrogant because his entire demeanor has shifted to cocky arrogance inside of the last five minutes.

"Go for it."

"I get the impression you are humoring me in some way because you keep glancing at your watch," he says directly. "Do you have somewhere better to be? Because I don't need you to do me any favors by gracing me with your presence."

My first reaction is relief because you can't force chemistry, and I'd have more fun standing in line at the post office. My second reaction happens simultaneously as he gets up, and I remember that weasel of a man pictured on Miles' phone.

"Wait," I start, as my arm shoots out to try and stop him from getting up. It has no impact on him and hardly slows him down.

"Enjoy the rest of your day," he scoffs. Then he heads for the door, and I'm chasing him like a jilted lover.

We are outside the coffee shop before he even realizes I'm at his heels. When I finally succeed in grabbing his inked-up arm and slowing him down, he spins around and turns on me like a slap to the face. Sudden and intense. His eyes are on fire, and he isn't interested in anything else I have to say.

"Stop. Please. Just wait." I'm not making any sense, but the contempt radiating off of him neutralizes any fight I have left and renders me near useless.

"Got something to say, Alabama?" he challenges. It sounds like a threat, but none so threatening as the face on Miles' phone.

"I can explain."

"Do it then, but I doubt I want to hear it. Prissy girls are *not really my style*," he hands me back my own words, but now they sound acidic.

***

"Are you fucking kidding me right now?" It's out of his mouth before I even finish explaining. His look of sheer disgust has filled the space around us and leaves me feeling kind of timid.

"You want me to date your pretentious ass for three months when I don't even want to have coffee with you again?" Now, he can't decide whether to laugh or stomp away from me. He settles on an exaggerated huff.

"Please? You would be doing me a favor."

"A favor? I don't even like you!" Under the weight of his glare, my skin starts to feel tight and itchy all over.

"Listen, as long as all the pretense is out of the way, I can actually be a nice person. That wasn't me back there. It was my response to doing something I didn't want to do."

"That sounds just as bad, Alabama!" his hatred comes back into crisp focus.

"Look at it this way, I *have* to be responsive to whatever you want to do. You will be driving the ship—you get to pick all the restaurants, no hassles fighting over the remote…it's all about you. Come on, a few texts a week and maybe a couple of hours on the weekends."

He scowls at me, completely unconvinced. Funny enough, I wouldn't mind hanging out with the guy, I just don't want to date him. He was nice at first, he was a gentleman, and he's not *bad* to look at, just not my type.

"I promise, I will be the most agreeable, doting, fake girlfriend anyone has ever had. And seriously, I'm not usually a bitch, I just felt railroaded by my friends, and you got caught in the crossfire."

"If I were to agree to this—which I'm not, you would seriously do whatever I want, *how* I want, no prissy attitude—ever?"

15

"Well, I'm not going to run naked through Downtown, but within reason, yeah."

"You realize if I agree to this, I'm going to have fun with it, right? I will push your stuck-up, holier-than-thou attitude to the outer reaches of your limit."

"Now you make it sound like I'm going to be your sex slave. I'm not signing up for th—"

"Oh, please. I'd have to *want* to sleep with you for that. And trust me, I don't."

"So, do we have a deal?"

"No, you crazy woman! I need to think about it first. And just for the record, *you* are not my type either. I don't even like redheads."

"Ok then," I say, feeling a little stung. "I guess I'll just wait to hear from you about another date."

He stares at me for like, ten seconds before he responds like a dropped bag of wet sand, "Why are you looking at me like that? I don't kiss on the first date."

Chapter 5

Gavin waited five solid days before responding to me, and when he finally did, it was with a cryptic text:

Gavin: *Saturday, 1:30. Dress warm. Text me your address.*

Now that the fateful Saturday is here, I can't get Ivy and Miles out of my place fast enough. I don't trust either of them to interact with Gavin now that he knows the score.

If I had known a ten-a.m. jaunt to the dog park with Miles and his dog, Brutus would saddle me with his company all day, I would have skipped it. I swear, it's like I have gum stuck to the bottom of my shoe, and I can't scrape it off. Miles and Brutus were bad enough, but when Ivy just happened to stop by, I knew it would take an act of Congress to get them out of my loft.

"I'm serious, you guys, it's too soon for you to meet him. We are still getting to know each other. You have to leave." I'm pleading with them now, but neither of them gives a shit.

"What better way is there to get to know someone than by meeting their friends?" Miles asks as he scoops all twelve pounds of Brutus into his arms and casually leans back on the couch.

"Miles is right, should we make popcorn?" Ivy asks as she plops down next to him. It just so happens that she likes the process of us picking a guy for her. We landed on someone perfect, but they have not yet met in person.

"Fine, but when he gets here, I'm not even going to buzz him in. I'll just run out, and you two will have to cry in your popcorn until next time." I spin around and march to the bathroom to take a shower.

Surprise, surprise, when I emerge from the bathroom wrapped in a towel, my outfit has been pre-determined and is laid out on my bed. Skinny jeans, a black crochet top that would be shockingly slutty without a black tank-top underneath, and four-inch high heels.

"I'm not wearing that," I say breezily as I round the wall that obscures my clothing racks. "For one thing, he said to dress warm, and for another, patent leather stilettos are hardly appropriate for a daytime date."

"What?" Miles exclaims, outright scandalized. "He won't be able to get the mental image of those shoes over his shoulders out of his head all day!"

"What do you know about high heels over your shoulders anyway, Miles?" Ivy laughs.

"What? That's hot. Even I can appreciate that."

"I'm not wearing heels. Or see-through shirts for that matter. God, Miles, you are worse than a pimp."

We end up compromising on jeans, a key-hole top that is sexier than I would like, and some wedge booties, but while I'm in the bathroom blow drying my hair with twenty minutes to spare, my friends buzz Gavin up. So, when I walk out of the bathroom announcing that I need to change my bra because you can see my nipples, I'm caught off guard.

Miles looks over to Gavin and, without missing a beat, says, "It's hard to find an outfit that properly accessorizes with nipples."

Gavin laughs at him, then jumps right on the bandwagon, "And I thought nipples were the new black." I cut my eyes at him, then grab my jacket off the hook before my friends can do any real damage.

To my absolute horror, Ivy returns from the kitchen area, and hands Gavin a beer before the three of them sit down on my sectional.

It's three against one, and I don't like my odds. Miles and Ivy have no idea I told Gavin everything, so this is going to get very uncomfortable.

"So, Gavin, Alabama tells us you own your own tattoo shop, and you do a lot of charity work down at the homeless shelter, is that right?" Ivy further breaks the ice, just enough for me to fall through.

"Did she now?" he says as he points his smirking eyes in my direction. If it wasn't clear before who his online conversations were with, it is now. "Actually, that doesn't surprise me at all because she couldn't stop talking about how much she loves to selflessly donate her time to similar worthy causes. In fact, did she tell you we are volunteering at the Rescue Mission next Saturday?"

"Is that right?" Ivy asks, probably wondering if brunch and pedicures are off the table now.

"Yeah, it's so nice to connect with another altruistic soul. She has such a *beautiful heart*," Gavin says, and I would believe his bright smile if he wasn't so full of shit.

"Eyes. I was going to say she has such beautiful eyes," Miles says. He's thinking about something, and I don't trust where he is going with it.

"But you are absolutely right, Gavin. She is *such* a giver," Miles finishes, then they all turn to look at me and catch me mid-eye-roll.

"Giver, yes. So, she must have told you that her company is going to sponsor my booth at the tattoo convention next month in LA, right? It's amazing to have such a generous sponsor."

"Now thaaat….is a steep promise," Miles glares at me undetected by the others. I don't know if he thinks I was over-selling myself, or he knows how hard it is to squeeze money from my company's CSR program, but either way, he smells deception.

"Are you ready, Gavin?" I ask as I take a step toward the door.

"Nah, let's hang out for a bit," he says as he turns toward Ivy. "I'm a *complete stranger* to your friends, and I feel like they should get to know me a little."

Miles laughs, "Believe me, you are no stranger to us. Not at all, buddy. Alabama can't stop talking about you. *I feel like we know you already.*"

After Miles' exaggerated response, I'm worried he's on to me, and it makes the saliva in my mouth reverse-swallow from the anxiety. Miles is sharper than anyone I have ever met before, and even though Gavin is *for sure* messing with me, I get the distinct impression Miles knows what's up and is joining the ranks.

"Awww, she can't stop talking about me? That's so cute." Gavin tilts his head at me and gives me the fakest, most condescending smile I've ever seen in real life.

"And I would have guessed that I wasn't her type at all. It's good to hear she's not *shallow* enough to judge a book by its cover and is excited to get to know me," Gavin finishes, only just now taking his accusing eyes off me and turning to look at Miles.

"*Trust me*, we are *all* excited to see how this plays out," Miles says without taking his eyes away from the blazing holes he is staring into my head.

As soon as the outside door snicks shut behind us, I'm aware Miles and Ivy are watching us from three floors up, so I decide to play it cool for the moment.

"Thank you."

"No, thank you—that was a lot of fun unpacking you in front of your friends like that. Do they even know what a cunt you are?"

It takes everything I have not to react to his insult. And under the watchful eyes of my friends, I casually take his hand. Even though he stiffens at the contact and reciprocates like his fingers are made out of wood, he doesn't yank his hand away.

"I'll let you have that one because I was nasty to you when we met, but don't ever call me a cunt again." I'm not aggressive when I say it, it's more about drawing a line. If I let him get away with talking to me like that without standing up for myself, he will assume it's ok and do it again.

He scoffs, "I've been thinking about this little proposition of yours," he says as he indicates with his other hand toward a black Dodge Charger parked across the street in a metered spot. "My original plan was to pick you up and take you to the shop so you could sit on your pompous ass all day while I worked."

"That sounds…amazing?" I attempt to sound agreeable, but I still recognize a threat when I hear one. This "date" is critical because I will need to do some serious damage control later with Miles, and it will be a ton easier if I can present him with a bona fide date, not just details about what the inside of Gavin's tattoo shop looks like.

"And I still will if you make any part of this arrangement insufferable for me, got it?" As if to make his point that much clearer, he flings my hand away like it's covered in warts, then opens my door like a perfect gentleman.

"Roger that," I say in the instant before the door slams shut. As he rounds his car, I wonder for the hundredth time since I filled him in on the situation, if the end justifies the means. I have no doubt he is going to treat me like shit just to make a point, and then dump me on my lying ass. Why subject myself to this?

I know the answer to that already, and it's that I would much rather contend with Gavin's psychological warfare than with Miles'.

"You look handsome," I try when he gets in. And he would—if he would cut his hair, shave his stubble, and wash off all his tattoos. He has that haircut from the prohibition era that is short on the sides and can look classy if he combed the top part back, but he doesn't, so he looks like he belongs in a grunge band instead of looking polished and well-groomed.

"Shut up."

His words and tone are completely dismissive, and I have a hard time dealing with conflict, so I look out the window instead of telling him to go suck a bag of dicks.

After what feels like hours but might equate to, like, six minutes, I find I can't take the silent treatment any longer. Plus, his choice of music is too base-heavy with the sub-woofer in the back. The only thing the ride has accomplished so far, is loosening the leftover phlegm in my lungs from my bout of walking pneumonia last year.

"So, what kind of tattoos do you do?" I ask, competing with the base that might actually be jiggling my cheeks.

"What, you mean beyond sorority letters and tramp stamps? What the hell do you mean, *what kind of tattoos do I do?*"

"Never mind, I just thought that tattoo artists specialized in something, like bio-mechanical, or new scho—"

"Portraits," he says like he just wants to shut me up, then moves his thumb slightly over the volume buttons on the steering wheel and turns up the music to discourage any more attempts at conversation.

I spend the rest of the ride calculating the cost for an Uber home, which is a lot because now we are way out by the stadium. I've learned my lesson about trying to talk to him, though, so I haven't made any further attempts.

I figure if I come home crying or seething with rage, my friends can't really consider it a success and couldn't possibly insist on a third date. Thankfully, I'm not masochistic enough to put myself through this again anyway. I'm also not going out with that other guy. I'm officially revoking my participation in this ludicrous intervention as of right now.

After he parks his growly car and unlatches his seatbelt, he looks over at me like he's expecting me to say something. The fresh new silence in the car is just as loud as the horrible music was. And now, he's just sitting there looking at me expectantly.

I'm not even sure what I *would* say because the last time I was in this part of town, it was for the circus, and I was twelve. So, I just raise my eyebrows at him and wait for further assholeness.

"Let's go, Princess," he says over his shoulder as he climbs out of his seat. I get out of the car like I'm about to face the firing squad and adjust my purse strap. He waits for me to catch up, but it's clear that neither one of us wants to be together.

I naively hoped Gavin would soften back into the smiling man I first met in the coffee shop, but it's clear that is not going to happen. So, I will have to slap a smile on my face and get through the next couple of hours with the petulant child.

I grew up in a politician's home, and the thing I learned above all else is that I can get through any situation if I have the right mask in place. That knowledge should serve me well today. I know just the one I need, the agreeable smile that covers my seething hatred.

Once we have stood in line quietly for a bit, with me eyeballing the crowd and trying to figure out what kind of event this is, Gavin hands me a ticket, and the mystery is solved.

Pit passes to the Monster Truck Rally.

Chapter 6

Once inside, the energy is frenetic, and the smell of exhaust tickling my nostrils is enough to make me cough a few times before I can get my face under control. It's cold too because evidently, the sponsors don't want the crowd to die of carbon monoxide poisoning, so they have all the barn doors to the arena open.

"Want to get a closer look? We have pit passes," Gavin says. His hard shell has maybe cracked a tiny bit because I can see the shiny excitement of a little boy in his eyes. He is definitely not smiling and still looks at me like I'd make a better speedbump for the trucks, but at least he is talking to me.

"Yeah, I do, but I need to go to the bathroom first. I can meet you in the pit if you don't want to wait for me," I offer. I'm trying to be as accommodating as possible as the crowd swells with the intensity and bubbling chaos of a mass salmon spawn. I figure it will be easier to find him in the pit rather than among the general masses that are currently overrunning the concession stands out here. Plus, if I leave him waiting by the ladies' room, his mood will continue to sour as the swell of people bumps and jostles him.

"Right, you need to wash your hands before touching a hotdog. Got it. I'll see you inside then." He turns and melts into the crowd. What a dick. I'm about to watch big trucks drive over dirt piles with a complete asshole. If anyone should be pissy, it's me.

When I find him in the pit, he is talking to one of the drivers who the fans are swarming for his autograph. I approach him gently, like he's a snorting bull ready to charge, and hand him a 24-ounce beer. He looks at me with complete befuddlement, which is kind of a good look on him because it strips him of his usual armor.

"What's a monster truck rally without a Budweiser?" I say by way of explanation before taking a sip of my own.

"Jace, this is Alabama. Alabama, Jace," Gavin says as he steps aside so we can shake hands easier. "Jace drives the Bay City Scythe, which is that beast right over there," he points to a massive black and red truck painted with rips and tears like it drove through a field of barbed wire.

"Your boy right here is no slouch either. I had to wait six months just to sit in his chair, and that was *with* tickets to offer," Jace says, as he tries to sign everything that is thrust in front of him, from hats and t-shirts, to photos, and boobs.

It is no exaggeration when I say that Jace is being overrun by squealing fans that want nothing more than to breathe the same gasoline infused air as him. So, Gavin and I say our goodbyes, then make our way over to a purple monster truck with a snarling mouth painted on it.

I'm only slightly taller than the wheels on these things. They are huge, and the paint job on each of them is incredibly intricate—To be completely honest, I'm a little surprised at how impressed I am right now.

***

Once it's time for the show to get started, we make our way to the front-and-center seats Gavin has secured for us. I've already peed twice, and by now, we are each on our second beer.

The first handful of events are the ATV and speedster races, followed by the obstacle courses. They are so fun and engaging to watch that when I get splattered by mud on my neck and cheek, I feel like I've been anointed by a redneck priest. After that, I get even more caught up in the testosterone-filled demonstration.

When I glance over at Gavin, he's smiling at the look of shock and awe on my face. He may even be a little surprised that I don't whip out some antibacterial wipes or hand sanitizer. His unguarded smile reminds me that he wasn't always an asshole. No, that was me.

I'm still not attracted to his grittiness, and he is a total bad boy, so that won't change, but at least we can have fun together—I mean, independently have fun, while sitting next to each other.

Right before the monster truck main event, I attempt to start a conversation again. It seems like a good time because Gavin was just as engaged as the rest of the crowd, and now he appears slightly more receptive to me.

"I think it's amazing that Jace wanted you to do his tattoo so bad that he waited six months. You must be a phenomenal artist." I purposely avoid scratching off the dried mud that now itches where it has tightened and clung to my skin. For the first time, I notice he has a few drops of cast-off mud as well, one on the outside corner of his upper lip, and two others on his temple. I love that he accepts its presence just like I did, it's like a joint baptism.

"I don't know about phenomenal, but I'm fairly well known for my portraiture work. Here comes Jace." Now, he sits back, finished with our conversation, and cheers right along with everyone else.

For the record, I don't blame him for hating me. If someone had done to me what I did to him, I would have contemplated slapping a bumper sticker for erectile dysfunction on the back of their car. The beauty in doing such a thing is that he wouldn't know whether it'd been on for five minutes or two months before he noticed it.

In hindsight, even if I still came clean about my friend's involvement in the date, I should never have stressed how much he wasn't my type. There is no recovering from bruising someone's self-esteem like that.

The truth is, I think this date was meant to punish me, and because I'm having a great time—all things considered, this will no doubt be our last. Unless that is, he does take me to his shop and sit me in the corner for nine hours.

One other thing I feel like I should point out is, even though he thinks I'm a snob, *he* is the one wearing Rag & Bone jeans, and I can promise you that I have never spent $250 on a pair of jeans.

***

When he drops me off, he pulls up in front of my building but makes no move to get out or even turn off his engine. This must be how butt-hurt guys drop off their dates at the end of the evening. Never mind the fact that we are in the heart of downtown, and there is a homeless person passed out on the ground not one block away from where Gavin's car currently idles.

Cognizant of the fact that I deserve his scorn, I attempt to leave him with a better impression of me because it will surely be his last.

"I had fun with you tonight, so thank you for humoring the situation and taking me out on a date," I say, and then realize that even though I was a horrendous date the first time we met, I still have some self-respect to defend.

"And for lowering your standards enough to take a not-your-type redhead out on a pretend date." There, I got in a reminder that he, too, took a swing in the beginning. I feel a bit vindicated by reminding him that I'm not the *only* nasty person in this car.

"We both lowered our standards tonight, didn't we? Have fun with the boring accountant your friends pick for you next. I'm sure vanilla sex and dinners at Applebee's will be more to your liking."

My mouth falls open, but true to form, I have no epic comeback. Not until I try to fall asleep later tonight anyway, then I will come up with dozens. Stunned by his audacity, I open the door in slow motion with my mind still reeling.

Before I shut the door behind me, and with my last grasp at retaining some dignity, I say, "Maybe your next portrait will be of a horse's ass, that should come really easily for you," then I shut the door before he can dismantle that comeback with a much better one of his own.

Truth be told, I like his fire. It makes me think he is not used to defending his worthiness. And while I'm being honest, the sexiest thing in the world to me is not a physical characteristic at all. It's confidence. Of which Gavin has a stadium's worth of.

The rickety old elevator in my building hasn't worked the entire two years I have lived here, so while I trudge up three flights of stairs, I weigh my options. Do I admit to my friends that I had a great time but that Gavin isn't interested in seeing me anymore? Or do I regale them with disappointing stories about what a jerk he is and hope they don't still deem him worthy of another date?

I don't have to wait too long to decide because when I step into my loft, I see Ivy still on my couch. My face must be pretty unreadable because her first question is, "Why are you home already? It's not even nine-thirty."

"I don't know, Ives. I had fun, but I'm getting the very distinct impression that he is not into me." Turns out, those words bother me more than I thought they would.

"Stop it. You are trying to sabotage this because he isn't a corporate mucky-muck, and you can't picture your wedding in the Hamptons with him."

"One. I would never get married in the Hamptons. And two. *I* had a great time, *he* is the one who cut the date short and all but high-fived me before getting the hell out of here. He hardly slowed the car down before pushing me out of it."

"Alabama, that man is ridiculously sexy. If you can't see that, I genuinely question your sanity. And not only that, his profile says he is looking for a serious relationship—Not a hook-up! Don't you see how perfect he is?"

"Ivy! I told you, it's him that's not interested in me."

"You are a liar, liar, pants-on-fire, lying liar. You are hung up on his tattoos and piercings, and you know it."

"You know about his piercings?"

"I mean...yeah." She suddenly looks shy, which gets me to wondering where his other one is.

"None of that even matters, Ivy. He is not going to contact me again."

"Since you are so resistant to reason, I'm going to show you something," she says as she flings the chenille throw off her legs, and stands up. I decide not to argue any further because she isn't listening anyway. She clearly thinks I'm pushing Gavin away instead of the other way around.

She pulls her laptop from her work bag and sits back down on the couch. While we are waiting for the screen to wake up, something occurs to me.

"Why are you still here, anyway? What if I would have brought him up for some rough and dirty sex? What then?" I ask pointedly.

"Alabama, you forget something very important. I've communicated with him a couple of weeks longer than you have, and in that time, I've gotten to know him pretty well. He would never have sex with someone after just one date." Her level of certainty about that is unsettling to me. In the weeks he was communicating with my friends, he was charming and open, and respectful. And perhaps more importantly, interested.

Now I'm starting to feel like I made a hasty decision. Maybe he is more my type than I initially thought. That realization can do nothing for me now, so a fat lot of good it does.

"I'm going to break the rules because I think you need to give this guy a chance, but if you tell Miles and Arden that I showed you his profile, you're dead to me—got it?"

***

The feeling in my stomach is what a pound of Pop Rocks and a two-liter of Coke must feel like, hot and hateful. I've spent well over an hour sifting through Gavin's dating profile and trying to convince Ivy that I didn't push him away—well, not like she thinks anyway. My conclusion is that he is witty, hilarious, thoughtful, and he cleans up really well.

There are a few pictures from his profile that sprinkle salt in the wounds of my newly discovered realization. They are, in no particular order, him drawing tattoos on the arm of a cancer patient at the Children's Hospital. Him, dressed in all pink at the Race for a Cure while kissing the cheek of his mother, presumably. And a *super*-hot one of him on a snowboard going off a jump while grabbing the edge of it. There is also a dapper picture of him in a suit with his hair combed back, and you can't even see the tattoo on the side of his neck. Lastly, there is one of him holding a toddler while both of them laugh in each other's face.

Apparently, the one with the kid had sparked the most online conversation between him and my friends because there is a lot of cute banter back and forth about his niece, and how impressed I was that he held her with such confidence instead of like she was a package about to detonate.

I still hate his tattoos. I do. And I could never bring him home to meet my parents. Also, while I'm busy clawing my way up the corporate ladder, he is selflessly volunteering his time at the Children's Hospital. There are a ton of reasons we don't fit.

We could never work.

But damn, he is kind of an awesome guy.

Chapter 7

It's been radio silence from Gavin for a week and a half, no surprise there, but you know who has not maintained radio silence? Miles. I keep trying to circumvent his arctic stare and his probing interrogation, but I can't avoid him forever. I've played the *work is kicking my ass right now* card on four different occasions, and now Miles is calling bullshit.

Working in his favor is also the simple fact that he knows the deadline for my looming Archimedes project was this morning. So, I'm currently having a hard time evading his latest text.

Miles: *Happy Hour at Lumiere, or your place. You make the call.*

Me*: Arden hates Lumiere.*

Miles: *Arden and Brady are celebrating three years of romantic bliss tonight. So, they will probably politely debate where to go eat and then go home for a rousing game of Scrabble.*

Me, still evading*: I thought Ivy was going out with that guy, Christopher tonight?*

Miles: *You mean, **Christian?** The guy **you** helped pick out for her?*

Me: *Yes, him.*

Miles*: Are you done?*

Me: *Huh?*

Miles: *Are you done avoiding me with your ridiculously amateur stall tactics?*

Me: *Not really.*

Miles: *See you at Lumiere at six. You're buying because this conversation took fifteen minutes that I'll never get back.*

***

Let me start by saying that Miles is my longest and most treasured friend. Let me also reiterate his freakish ability to strip a situation down to exactly what it is. In short, I love him—but I'm also kind of afraid of him right now.

My nervousness that he knows what I did is not at all irrational. It's also not at all soothed by the reckless intake of blood orange vodka martinis, which sound more like an ominous foreshadowing than a signature drink. I'm on my second when he finally joins me at the bar.

When he hugs me, I see the softer side of him that perhaps really does miss seeing me. When he fixes his eyes on mine, I know I've terribly miscalculated.

"What are you drinking?" I ask, I already know what he will order, but I'm trying to steer the conversation away from his accusations. Miles never beats around the bush. So if he has something to say, you better brace yourself for it.

"Cut the shit," he snorts out a laugh because *he knows*, I know that he knows.

"Alright, but first tell me how you figured it out," I say as I push the bar menu to the side and prepare to be amazed.

"Are you serious right now? I interacted with the guy on your behalf for weeks before you entered the picture like a box of lit firecrackers. His entire demeanor has changed." The bartender puts a pint of beer in front of him that he didn't even have to order and then gives a somewhat stealthy wink. At this stage of the game, Miles almost expects this type of treatment, and not for the first time, I find myself wondering if his sense of entitlement has rubbed off on me a little bit.

"Your turn," he says, "Tell me why you told him. And then tell me how you still managed to pull off a date with him because this sounds like a story I need to hear to believe."

"As to *why,* there are a bunch of reasons. You know my family. Coming from a political family, there are certain expectations of me, and you know as well as anyone how much of a microscope I'm under."

"I'm still not convinced."

"Ok then, how about my career? I negotiate the exclusivity contracts now. My boss expects me to wine and dine the big-wigs of these massive accounts—which sometimes includes dinners with my significant other. Can you imagine how they would question my credibility if my boyfriend is sitting across from them with a tattoo up his neck and his tongue pierced?"

"That's not all he has pierced," Miles says smugly before he re-directs the conversation back to my shortcomings. "So, let me get this straight, you are saying you'd rather date someone with a Country Club membership, and his fucking collar popped because he would represent you better to your family and your corporate accounts?"

"Uhhh, well, it sounds really shitty when you put it like that."

"It is shitty. Ask yourself this. Where would I be today if I let society define me instead of being self-actualized enough not to give a shit how other people see me."

"I don—"

"Tell me!" he demands. I'd say he's angry, but I know him better than that. He is hurt.

"Number one, you'd date women," I try for humor, but it slides right off him because he thinks I've missed the point.

35

"You know what my mom told me a long time ago? It was the most profound thing to come out of her mouth, and it plays in my head like an anthem. She, as you know, knew I was gay before I truly understood it myself, and she wanted to instill something in me for when I did start to question my sexuality." I smile wistfully because Miles hit the jackpot when it comes to moms.

"She said, *lions don't concern themselves with the opinions of sheep*," he pauses to let that sink in, then he goes in for the kill. "If you make your life choices based on what you think people expect of you, then you deserve the life you end up with, Alabama. No one else is living your life for you. Why the hell would you factor them into your decisions?"

Then he twists the knife in my ribs when he adds, "I love you, but you are a fucking idiot, and I have never been so disappointed in you."

His words resonate with me as they land. When I switch the circumstances, I realize I've always pushed him to be true to himself. I've been the first into battle with him in defense of loving whoever he wants to. I'm not sure why the same convictions don't apply to me. Maybe because I figure if I don't date someone perceived as unsavory, then I'll never fall in love with someone I would *have* to defend.

Full disclosure, I'm pretty disappointed in myself as well. After letting the slap of his words fade a little, I say the only thing I can at this juncture.

"How do I fix it?"

Chapter 8

Miles' solution to my dilemma was both incredibly simple and ridiculously far-fetched. Plus, my life would have to be spinning wildly out of control for me to permanently mar my body in the same way that had spun me in the other direction when I met Gavin. *Get a tattoo*, he said, as if he were suggesting a mid-day coffee. And though he thought it was a perfectly feasible option, I took a hard pass. Really, anything short of tattooing 'hypocrite' across my forehead would never work.

I can, however, engage Miles' plan B, which is to bring Gavin lunch at his shop. Even though my knees are practically knocking together with nervousness, I figure it's the only thing I can do that wouldn't earn me the middle finger of his right hand.

So, here I am using my own lunch hour to bring him a turkey sandwich and cup of soup from my very favorite deli. Never mind that I have wasted nothing short of twenty minutes sitting in my car trying to summon enough courage to walk in there, and now the soup is probably cold and the sandwich soggy.

When I push open the door, I notice two things right away, one— it's loud. The music has a presence all its own, and it's a dominating one. And two, it's bright and clean. The furniture up front, as well as the reception desk, is chic yet industrial. The design is something you would expect to see in an art gallery or trendy salon. Adorning the walls are huge framed pieces of art—tattoo art, but like nothing I've ever seen before. I can tell they are drawings, but the realism in each one makes them seem three-dimensional and freakishly alive.

"Can I help you?" the receptionist asks politely. She has a ring through her nose like a bull, and heavy makeup, but her demeanor is still young and sweet.

"Yeah, um. Hi. I was hoping to talk to Gavin…if he has a minute?" The words sound like they've been punched out of my chest, and if it's possible for teeth to vibrate, mine do.

"He is with someone, but I can poke my head into his room and see if he has a second." She turns to walk away but stops herself and asks, "Can I get you anything? Chai tea? Cappuccino? Sparkling water?"

"I'm good. Thanks." Honestly, I would have been less surprised to be offered a shot of whiskey than a cappuccino. To me, tattoo shop branding seems more bad-ass than anything polite or fitting of a Chai tea or sparkling water.

She walks away to let Gavin know someone is here to see him, but before she branches off into one of the rooms, she evidently sees him in the back of the shop. I hear her call out, "Oh good, you're not gloved. Someone wants to talk to you. Do you have a minute?"

Then she waves me back, "Come on, he's at the printer."

As I walk, I try to remember that I'm doing something nice for him, but overriding that fact, is the memory of calling him a horse's ass the last time I saw him.

The receptionist smiles as she passes me on the way back to her post, and I take a few more steps toward Gavin. His back is to me while he pushes buttons and then waits for something to print. He doesn't seem the least bit curious who has dropped by to see him—that, or he doesn't care.

"I thought I would bring you some lunch as a peace offering." My voice starts off timid but gains strength by the time I finish speaking. He still doesn't turn around, but he does look to the ceiling as if praying for the strength to deal with me.

"You mean you're not here for a massive tattoo?" he asks as he finally turns around to look at me.

"Noooo, I just wante—"

"Maybe a piercing then? Do you think poking a hole through your body will deflate your giant ego? No, probably not," he answers himself as he reaches toward the machine to retrieve his printout. I can't tell what the image is, but the stencil is pretty big.

I don't respond, but it's not because of his insult. A tattoo is outside the realm of possibilities, but...

"I already ate, but you can give that to Christy on your way out," he says dismissively as he walks away from me.

"Sure, yeah, and I'll just make my appointment when I give her your cast-off sandwich," I say, and it stops him in his tracks. He pauses before facing me again.

"I'm not tattooing you. Make your appointment with one of the other artists. Scott is only booked a couple of weeks out."

"I'm not getting a tattoo," I say.

"Well then, all of our piercers are great. You should be in good hands." Then he disappears into one of the tattoo rooms, and I try to rapid-blink away the tears that have arrived unannounced. I haven't teared up over a guy since Todd Bernhardt, and that was sophomore year in high school.

Gavin's whole persona is on the opposite end of the spectrum from the thoughtful guy who draws tattoos on kids with cancer and kisses his mom on the cheek. I'm not saying I don't deserve it, I'm just saying it is a rough lesson.

And now I have to get pierced.

***

Another week goes by before I have to face the fact that my piercing appointment is on the immediate horizon. As in, today, after work. I've been in a sort of denial about its approach, but I can't avoid it any longer. Which means I have to decide where I will be puncturing my flesh. The piercing itself is just to prove I can. Then I plan to remove the jewelry and let the hole in my body, as well as my spitefulness heal over.

The decision of where to pierce my body is proving difficult. I figure ears are too typical, and I can't do my face for the same reason I can't date Gavin, so no lip, brow, or nose. My lady bits and nipples are so far off the table that I hardly spare them a thought. Pretty much that leaves me with my belly button, and Gavin already made fun of sorority letters and tramp stamp tattoos, so I'm sure he feels the same about belly rings.

I don't even know why I'm factoring him into my decision, he has tattoos booked out a year from now and has hired people to do the piercings, so I probably won't even see him. I would cancel the appointment altogether were it not for two very important things. One, my pride. And two, I have a monetary donation from my company for his damn tattoo convention. I'll just leave the check along with my dignity behind when I leave. Pierced.

The donation wasn't easy to come by, but re-wording *tattoo shop owner* into *young business professional* finally did the trick. I'm assuming it's not nearly enough to cover his costs, but at least I kept my word—or more accurately, his word on my behalf. My company is not exactly sponsoring his booth at the tattoo convention, but he should at least know I tried to squeeze blood from a turnip.

This morning I decided to stay late at work so I could go straight to my appointment, but only because running home to primp first made no sense. I scheduled with Lillianna, who, according to the receptionist is the best piercer they have, and I don't expect to see Gavin at all, so I figured my executive work attire would be fine. That was this morning.

As the day trudged on, I felt less and less like strutting into a tattoo shop wearing corporate clothes and three-inch heels. If my reputation as a stuffy, judgmental bitch precedes me at all, then walking in like this would be admitting the truth of it just as much as shouting it through a megaphone.

The truth is, I *am* a stuffy, judgmental bitch. My parents molded me into one so fluidly and consistently that I didn't see it happening. I was raised under the thumb of a powerful politician and bathed regularly in pretense and hypocrisy. If I ever had a wayward thought, they snuffed it out before it ever came to fruition. And since birth, they made every decision for me and coaxed every move through a refining filter.

Once somewhat freed from the distillation process that was my life, and sent away to college—to follow my predetermined path without hope of the slightest variation, I began to recognize my own thoughts. The most damaging of which was that I hated the puppet I had become. I hated myself.

The darkest time of my life was when I recognized the qualities I loathed in my parents as my own. To this day, when I see a glimmer of my mother or father in myself, I want to soak in an acid bath and start anew.

That is the reason I hustle so hard in my career. I work twice as hard as anyone in my department, and I always will. I feel a compulsive need to carve myself as my own entity and to never, *ever* rely on my parents for anything.

The very idea of this piercing tickles at the rebellion I feel on every surface of my skin, but astonishingly, I still deeply crave my parent's acceptance. Their indoctrination runs deep, so there is a painful push and pull going on inside of me. On one hand, I don't want to be anything like them. On the other hand, I don't know how not to be like them.

The healthiest aspect of my life has always been my friends. It's through them I learned about love and trust, as well as such esoteric concepts as basic integrity, and respect—for others as well as myself. My child and young adulthood were developed and refined around the mentality of a business arrangement instead of a nurturing environment, and I will *never* be free of the consequences of it.

I wonder how much of this desire to change Gavin's impression of me is due to the potent *need* to scrape off the remnants of my parent's stronghold. I can still hear their echo in my prejudice, and I want to gnaw off the part of them that still resonates with me.

I don't blame Gavin for hating me. I still hate parts of myself. And I certainly don't disagree with his assessment of me. It's spot on. But for some reason, I refuse to let this go. Which is the long version of why I'm keeping my appointment at his shop.

Chapter 9

If I didn't know better, I would think I was about to have a facial at an uptown spa. The piercing room is, dare I say—soothing? Three of the walls are crisp white, and the fourth has thin, rough slats of stacked limestone covering it in varying shades of white. There is a fountain burbling away in the corner of the room, an oil diffuser emitting a fine mist scented with lavender, and a shallow pot of leafy bamboo reeds tied together with red and gold ribbon.

The single piece of framed art on the wall is a drawing of Buddha that looks so authentic and alive I half expect it to wink at me. The quiet music fits with the Zen-like atmosphere but sounds more like a meditative chant than a song. The two pieces of furniture in the room are a spa chair, currently in the upright position, and a cabinet that looks like a mandala was hammered out of chrome and then wrapped around it.

My piercer, Lillianna, is also not what I expected. She has long, silky blonde hair and moves like a ballerina—purposely, yet with an undefined grace. She has no visible tattoos, no stretched out earlobes, no cold stare or look of future regret. She does have a spattering of piercings, though.

Her piercings are different from any I have seen before because they are on flat parts of her body and look more like a glued-on rhinestone or silver ball. Four such silver balls run along the underside of her left collarbone and look almost pretty—delicate even. Another five or six balls are placed up the outside edge of her right forearm like ants marching in a row. Scratch that—both of her forearms have the same row of balls, not only the right one. Then she has a line of three rhinestones in her cleavage and a single one in the middle of her top lip, right above her cupid's bow.

She directs me to have a seat on the spa chair as she takes the clipboard of paperwork, waivers, and post-care instructions from me and then begins to read over it. After seeing her piercings, I no longer want to ask for a belly ring. It seems like the navel piercing ship has sailed and another, more sophisticated one has docked in its place. She doesn't even have her ears pierced.

"Can I answer any questions or address any concerns for you, Alabama?" she asks. Her eyes are kind and have an almost heroic glint to them, it puts me at ease somehow.

"I guess my only concern now is that after seeing your piercings I kind of want one like that instead of what I originally thought I wanted," I say, sounding, as well as feeling incredibly stupid.

"This kind of piercing," she explains, while the tips of her fingers feather over the balls beneath her collarbone, "Is called a surface piercing. They are a little more invasive than a traditional piercing because they traverse more skin, but they are beautiful. Actually, the client right before you had me do one on the nape of her neck. She chose a rather large piece of jewelry, so the gauge and ends of the barbell were bigger than I normally recommend starting with, but she knew what she wanted, and she's not new to piercings, so I allowed it."

While I'm chewing over the words, *more invasive*, someone knocks on the door. When they push it open, the aggressive base-driven music invades Lillianna's serene piercing room, spits in its mouth and then beats it to death. Worse than the music, Gavin now dominates the space as he closes the door behind him, effectively shutting out the racket he calls music. That door must be something special to ward off all that noise.

He nods at me, somewhat of an acknowledgment, I suppose, and then speaks directly to Lillianna. "Lil, I need a favor." He is wearing a white dress shirt with the sleeves rolled up and some faded, ratty jeans that I know he bought like that because they are too perfectly distressed to be genuinely old and beat-up.

"What do you need?" she asks, not at all concerned that he just barged in on her consultation with me.

"Christy can't go to L.A with me this weekend anymore. I'm desperate."

"Gavin, I'm a single mother. What about the twins?" she looks sympathetic to his plight, but that's all.

"I'll pay for a babysitter. I'll pay double."

"I've never left them with anyone but my mother. I can't find some random babysitter and then trust them with my babies for three days." I love that she conveys what a ridiculous suggestion it is with a little laugh mixed into her refusal.

"I'll pay your mo—"

"Gavin, I can't go. I'm nursing, and even if I pumped all weekend, there is nowhere near enough milk on hand at home." Then she pokes his chest and adds, "What did you think those daily bags of breastmilk in the fridge were for?"

"What, that's not coffee creamer?" he teases. I remember when he was smiley and cracking jokes with me. Now he has frozen over, so seeing his personality shine with someone else makes me more than a little regretful.

"I'll figure it out. What are you piercing, Alabama?" He changed gears so fluidly, it takes me a second to realize he is talking to me. I can't tell if there is a challenge hidden in his question, but I scramble anyway because I still haven't decided, and I refuse to tell him *my belly button.*

"She is thinking about a surface piercing, but I've only just collected her paperwork, so we haven't gotten that far yet." It almost sounds like she is coming to my aid, and I like her even more for her intercession.

"Alright then, have fun," he says before the pounding base swallows him back into the shop.

"I didn't realize you two knew each other. I'm surprised he didn't offer his opinion," Lillianna says, not without affection.

"We've met before," I leave it at that, and then ask, "Why would he offer his opinion anyway? Why would he care what I pierce?"

"Oh, he has his favorite spot. Trust me, all guys do."

"What's his favorite spot?" I ask, but I'm not even sure I want to know, and I damn sure don't want it to get back to him that I asked.

"He likes surface piercings right here," she drags a fingernail diagonally up her abdomen almost to her hip. The section she indicates is almost intimate. Or, in my case, the exact spot I nearly tattooed with a rose on a drunken dare back in college. More accurately, I was aiming for a *fuck you* tribute to my parents—but thankfully, I was too drunk, and they promptly turned me away. That piercing *would* look pretty sexy, but I'm not sure I'm up for multiple surface piercings tonight. I would need to give it more thought.

"What's your pleasure?" she asks, and I suppose she refers to the sacrificial patch of skin I will be offering up because undoubtedly, one knows such things when entering her piercing studio.

"Um," is all I can push past my teeth, and it leaves me sounding dumber than I look—which is super dumb as I swing my feet nervously beneath me, like a child waiting for a round of immunizations. *Don't say belly button, don't say belly button.* "My ears," I finally spit out, not yet ready for a more invasive surface piercing.

"Your ears?" Lillianna asks as she pulls something from the shelf and then approaches me with a well-worn leather portfolio. She leans a hip against the edge of the spa chair where I sit, effectively erasing any personal space boundaries I may have come in with.

"That still leaves us with lots of options." As she flips through the pages, she creates a breeze that rustles her hair and teases the air with the scent of baby lotion. I think it's sweet that she has twin babies at home, but I kinda hate her for bouncing back the way she obviously has. Her waist is tiny, and I'd bet my right ovary that her tits are still perky.

My eyes land on one picture in particular. I've never seen someone's ear pierced the way the photo shows, and it's pretty. I might even get away with keeping it for a while at work.

"I like this," I say as I point to the image. There is a vertical line of three silver balls right where the top of her ear meets the side of her head. They decrease in size from small, to tiny, to really tiny. I like it, and that knowledge surprises me more than you know.

"That's called a triple forward helix. It's beautiful, good choice. You get to pick the jewelry. Anything from stainless steel ball studs, to spikes, to gems. I won't pierce you with hoops, though, they are too easily infected. So, if you want hoops, come back once you're all healed, and I'll switch them out for you." She leaves my personal space to retrieve a black velvet display with different sizes and shapes of jewelry. She needn't bother. I already know what I want.

"I want the clear jeweled ones, as small as you can get away with at the top and increasing in size toward my ear canal." I'm happy to have decided, but now—now, the fear of pain sets in, and my palms slick over.

***

I'm so relieved to have made it through *three* piercings without my face bouncing off the floor that I hardly flinch at the exorbitant cost of such a thing. The sharp pain of a needle passing through my cartilage once, twice, and a sadistic third time has dulled to the heat of a fire-breathing dragon. In fact, I think it's the pain endorphins that cloud my judgment and make me walk toward the buzz of a tattoo machine.

When I look into the room, Gavin is on a rolling stool facing me, but his client is between us, so he doesn't see me right away. The burly man has earbuds in, and his eyes closed against what must be the searing pain of the tattoo machine. He is sitting on the adjustable leather chair with his back to Gavin and a stoic look on his face.

"How did it go?" His question follows the abrupt halt of the buzzing machine, and it takes me a second to realize he is asking me about my appointment. He must see the throb of the piercings radiating off my ear like flashing emergency beacons.

Before I gather my wits enough to answer him, he addresses his client, who has just plucked the earbuds from his ears, "This is Alabama. She just had her clit pierced, so that's why she's aimlessly standing there shifting her weight. She's trying to stave off the orgasm that her jeans are trying to create by rubbing up against her swollen piercing." He delivers his statement as if he were announcing his tax deadline or something equally banal, then returns to his work.

"Your clitty, huh?" the man asks. I ignore both him and Gavin's dismissal with more shifting of my weight and then go over the falls in a barrel.

"I'll go to your convention with you."

Gavin abruptly rolls back from his canvas, spinning the casters of his stool in a sharp and uncharacteristic motion. He puts his tattoo machine on the surgical tray and then stares at me while holding both gloved hands up—possibly in a defensive boxing position. He doesn't say anything. He just cocks his head and squints his eyes at me, the gesture clearly saying what he won't. *What the hell did you just say?*

"Yeah, text me what I should pack. And a list of responsibilities I'll have while I'm there. And you have to handle my flight, I'll cover my hotel room, but you have to pay for the last-minute flight." I finish speaking before I have fully processed what I just committed to and then spin around to leave before I can recant the last minute of meandering speech.

Thirty minutes later, right before I pull into my parking garage, I hear a chime from my purse indicating an incoming text. It took Gavin all this time to chew on it, but he swallowed it just the same. It makes me smile because I know he has accepted his fate. He needs my help. He *had* to respond.

Once I hike up three flights of stairs and collapse on my couch with a bag of frozen peas—generally reserved for puffy eyes following a night of drinking, I read the text.

Arrogant Dickhead: *We fly out this Friday at 6:55am on United flight 5290. Return Monday 10:05pm, flight 7518. Pack clothes, a toothbrush, and a ball gag. I'll go over your responsibilities on the flight. It will mostly be consent forms and post-care. You won't be sterilizing anything like Christy normally does.*

Then, after further consideration, he shoots off another text.

Arrogant Dickhead: *I appreciate it.*

He doesn't exactly say thank you. Or concede that I'm saving his ass at the risk of losing my position at work because of the horrendously important meeting I will have to miss on Friday. The meeting is with a potential client that has such deep pockets you can hear the wind howling through the caverns. It's an account I have been courting for the last six months, and missing it is akin to jumping straight off the career ladder and breaking both ankles. Between you and me, I was hoping *convention this weekend,* meant this weekend—as in Saturday and Sunday.

Shit.

Wait.

Did he say, pack a *ball gag*?

Chapter 10

I had to work late tonight to salvage my potential client by suggesting dinner instead of the agreed upon office sit-down tomorrow. But the *true* test of my gall will come when I submit my expense report. In my defense, this account is massive. Therefore, I had to handle it with what the US government would consider *shock and awe*. Especially because I had to jockey our meeting around so I could meet with them before I leave town with Gavin. If they sign with us, there won't be a problem, if not—I shudder to think.

Right now, Miles is strewn across my bed like a snow angel, but the peaceful, serene imagery that may invoke stops there. He happens to be a very demanding snow angel and has some very clear ideas of how this weekend should go. Namely, me being a hussy and working my way into Gavin's good graces by way of his penis.

"See? Look at this," he insists, as he tosses his phone to the end of my bed and then sits up on his elbows. I pick up the phone and see a picture of a group of scantily clad women all covered in tattoos. One is completely topless—unless you count the ink across her chest. Never mind that it happens to be a Bald Eagle with each of her boobs clutched in its talons.

He seems to think this weekend will be one long seduction, but he is grossly underestimating how badly I pissed Gavin off. That, or he possesses a really inflated idea of my ability to seduce someone.

When he empties my lingerie drawer onto my bed and begins rifling through it with his big ole' man hands, I jump in.

"Miles, I have my own hotel room. When do you propose Gavin would see any of this? Plus, I was planning on sleeping in period underwear and sweatpants."

"No, Ma'am." He crosses his arms over his chest as if he actually needs to tell me not to pack period underwear. "You will do this my way. I mean it, Alabama—Down to the l-e-t-t-e-r. Now, where is your leather halter-top?"

"You mean, my ninja-assassin Halloween costume top?" I ask incredulously, but the bite of it softens with my yawn. When I think back to how the other women in his shop dressed, they were hip, yet professional. Sexy, but understated. I guess my leather halter top would work if I wear it with jeans.

"Yes—And Oooooh, get your roller derby costume too! Fishnets and hot pants, yes please," he says, excited by the dress-up possibilities enabled by my Halloween bin. I'll let him have his fun because it is futile to fight him on this right now, but if he thinks I'm going anywhere with Gavin dressed as Harley Quinn or a Viking warrior woman, he needs to adjust his dose.

"Miles, I'm tired, and I have to get up in five hours. I'll take the ninja-assassin top, but leave everything else in my suitcase alone." He nods, one quick motion to say he is taking my request under advisement, but I'm not delusional enough to think he won't get his way by adding some fishnets and vinyl.

"Trust me, ok? He thinks you are a high and mighty, judgmental, bitch with a vanilla sex life. I think he might be wrong about the vanilla sex, though—because I'm not gonna lie, I did play with the Ben Wa balls I found in your underwear drawer for a minute or two." He arches an eyebrow that could be misconstrued as condescension, except I know him well enough to read it for what it is— pride.

"And I still have a vivid memory of you hocking a loogy into the drink of that guy who called me a *faggot*—so, I'm relatively sure you aren't overly judgmental. But you *are* high and mighty."

"Miles!"

"Just calling it like I see it."

"Yeah, thanks for that," I say with a laughing eye-roll that belies the derision I should feel.

"Any-hoo, it is *our* job to remind him how compatible you are. But you won't have much time or many opportunities to change his mind, so you better get on board." Then he asks without pausing, "You have a garter belt, right?"

***

The whir of the plane's engines is enough to taunt me with the irony that I am flat exhausted, yet somehow pre-programmed not to be able to sleep on airplanes. Also grating on my nerves is the fact that I have to sit in a cloud of Cheetos dust because of the fervor in which the aisle seat occupant is bulldozing them into his mouth.

To make matters worse, Mr. Isle Seat keeps trying to make polite conversation, which is made *less* polite by his artificial cheese breath. It isn't enough to simply not inhale when engaged in conversation with him. I have to turn my back to the guy as though Gavin desperately needs my attention. To make matters *much* worse, is the fact that Gavin has earbuds in and doesn't give two shits about my distress signal.

He has already covered my responsibilities, which include checking IDs, getting release forms signed, and going over the post-care instructions with the finished clients. He also showed me his scheduling software, informed me how to book future appointment time slots based on the size of the piece, and how to collect deposits for those appointments.

As an afterthought, he also covered Christy's usual responsibilities that I will *not* be trusted with, including the use of the Autoclave, and prepping his space and instruments with barrier film.

He had explained the importance of a sterile environment and used terms such as *bloodborne pathogens, biohazard containers,* and *germicidal solutions.* All with the evangelical zeal of a prophet. Then, promptly ignored me to watch the vastness of the sky out his window.

In another attempt to send up a rescue flare, I try again to engage him in anything that keeps my back to the Cheetos guy. "Gavin," I say with exaggerated seriousness, "If you are thankful *at all* for my presence, you will get up to use the restroom and then come back and ask for the middle seat."

"Nobody actually *wants* the middle seat, Alabama."

"So, am I to understand that you are *not* grateful that I dropped everything to come help you—out of the pure goodness of my heart?"

"Not enough to take the middle seat."

"Ok. Then give me your earbuds."

"No."

"Slip this guy a Xanax?"

"How about I slip you a Xanax?"

***

The next time he speaks to me, it's in the Uber, and his words make the back of my neck hot enough to melt down my spine.

"Where are you staying? We'll drop you off first," he says without even glancing up from his phone.

"What do you mean, *where am I staying?*" There must be visible blotches of anxiety across my face as his meaning sinks in. Now, he *does* look up.

"Which hotel should we drive you to?" Realization is starting to prickle at him too. "Alabama, please tell me you booked a hotel room."

"Why would *I* book it? This is your deal. I don't even know where the convention is....LA is a big place, Gavin."

"You told me you would *cover the hotel.* Did you not?" Now he is kind of pissed, and I'm not sure he has any right to do anything except convey his utter gratitude in every word and action. I did harpoon my career just to help him out.

"As in, I will pay for it," I over annunciate each word. Since when does covering something mean setting it up?

He lets out a huge sigh and then tells the somewhat impatient Uber driver to stick with the original plan and take us to his hotel. "It's probably better to book rooms in the same hotel anyway," he says reasonably. Then adds, just to be a dick, "*Jesus,* Alabama."

Things go from bad to worse when the overly chipper woman at the front desk says, "I'm sorry, Mr. Rhodes, there are multiple conventions in town this weekend. We are all booked up." Then she adds, with a flirty smile and lipstick-smeared teeth, "Although, I do have some openings on Sunday night."

"No worries. We are in a sprawling city. I'll find something online," I say diplomatically, then turn to him, unclench my teeth and say, "Just text me where and when to meet you." Without letting out my breath, I turn and roll my suitcase toward the swanky hotel bar. It's not yet ten in the morning, but I need a stiff drink.

***

After perhaps an hour of pure frustration and no availability under $500 a night within a twenty-mile radius of the convention center, I do the only thing left to do. I place my forehead against the bar and hold my breath, so I don't cry.

I wanted to do something nice for Gavin because I'm still really ashamed of how I treated him, but all I'm doing now is coming off pathetic. I brought him lunch, I ran to his shop to get pierced, and I all but threw myself onto a plane with him. And now, *now,* it looks like I'm trying to share his hotel room too. My only options at this point are to cut my losses and go home, or pony up almost two grand for a last-minute room.

"Ready for another? You look like you might need one," the bartender asks the top of my head. I've learned his name is Sam and he is a part-time actor. He has thick, luxurious hair—and is handsome without the distraction of his overly hairy knuckles.

"I don't think you have enough liquor back there to make me feel better." My voice sounds muffled, but I'm not ready to sit up yet, not without first making a decision.

"Couldn't find a room?"

"Nope. Not without paying a king's ransom for it or picking up hepatitis in a crack house."

"You could stay with me. I'm sure that sounds skeevy as hell, but my roommates won't mind." I finally sit back and process his words. Is it crazy to admit I'm actually considering his offer? Do other violent crime victims have this same moment when they wonder if this is the bad decision that will turn them into a statistic?

"I mean...we only shoot gang-bang porn on Tuesdays and Wednesdays," he says with a deadpan delivery as he drops a skewer of green olives into my fresh martini. "So, you should be good." When I slowly meet his eyes, he is grinning from ear to ear.

"Gang-bang porn, huh?" Gavin says from behind me as he pulls out the heavy, regal stool to my left. Of course, *that* is the part he heard—not the part about Sam moving out here from Minnesota so his ailing mother could live in a warmer climate before she passed away five months ago. Or the part about him chasing his dream of becoming a voice-over actor.

"Uh. Sorry, man. I was just playing—I didn't mean any disrespect to your girl," Sam says as he takes a half-step back from me like he's about to get punched.

"It's all good. I like a good gang-bang as much as the next guy," Gavin says with a smile in his voice. He doesn't happen to correct Sam about me *not* being his girl, though, so Sam is still cautious.

"Did you find a place?" Gavin asks as he reaches for my dirty martini and takes an entitled sip before placing it back in front of me.

"Yes?" I say. It sounds like a question because it is. I'm looking at Sam for confirmation as he carefully nods his head after looking away from Gavin and then back to me.

"Great. I need to go get everything set up at the convention center and get back with enough time to shower before the doors open at 3:00. Want to come with? I could use some help hanging up the banner." Sure, *now* he is nice, but only because he wants my help.

Interrupting my indifferent shrug, he spits out, "Oh, crap. I left our wristbands in my room. I'll be right back."

It's not until he is fully out of the bar that Sam breathes again. I save him the torment by saying, "He's not my boyfriend. In fact, he is not even my friend."

"Thank, Christ. I thought he was going to crack my jaw. And, Alabama, seriously, my face is too pretty to be decked by a man with guns like that." We both laugh, and for the first time, I give some serious thought to Gavin's *guns*. With his muscles and tattoos, he must be intimidating to strangers, but I don't think of him as ferocious because I saw his tender side when we had coffee. Not since, mind you—but I know he is a good man.

He puts my mobile number into his phone and then shoots me a text, so I'll have his. Though he is clearly serious, I give him an out anyway. "Are you sure this is ok? I feel really weird about it because I don't want you to feel obligated in any way."

"Believe me, it's fine. I'll even text my roommate ahead of time so he can wash some dishes first," he smiles, and I weigh the fact that he took care of his sick mom against the fact that Ted Bundy was really charming too.

"You can have my room. I'll take the couch," *is he trying to entice me?* "Come on, don't look so conflicted. My door has a lock on it," he winks, but it's not in a lecherous way. It's more disarming than anything. *Kind of like Ted Bundy.*

"Thank you, Sam," I say as I put some cash on the bar for the drinks that I *should* be charging to my room.

"Just drop your luggage at the bell stand on your way out. They will store it until you're ready for it. Otherwise, text me when you finish up over there."

"It's really sweet of you to help me out. I'll search for a room again tomorrow, so hopefully, I'll only put you out one night." What I don't say is that I will be searching again in five minutes, and if I have my way, I won't be putting him out at all.

Gavin's back now, but his face is so entranced in the artificial glow of his phone that I'm not even sure he notices me make my way toward him. My feet feel heavy, kind of like they are full of needless bullshit—oh, wait…they are.

***

His booth is just big enough for a portable massage table with a rolling stool for him, a cabinet for his supplies, a tiny table for me with his laptop for scheduling purposes—no chair, and an eight-foot table where I currently arrange autographed prints, promotional stickers for his tattoo studio, and some very egotistical hats and t-shirts with his name on them. He already showed me how to use the appointment software and explained how to use the little square device on his phone that you insert a credit card into to pay for merchandise sales.

"How did you get all this stuff here?" I ask, not really expecting an answer because he is busy covering the massage table in plastic, but I'm curious just the same.

"I shipped it ahead of time." Then he asks, "Is there anything so far that you are uncomfortable with?"

What I keep to myself is, *you mean, besides the possibility of crashing somewhere that probably equates to a frat house—with a complete stranger?* But what I say is, "I don't think so. Appointments are easy, payments are easy, I know the aftercare instructions as well as my name…I should be good."

"I'll be right here the whole time, so you can always ask if you have questions, but it will be insane, so be prepared for that." He tucks his head and gets back to work wrapping the procedure table as if done communicating and already trying to forget I'm here.

"What qualifies as insane?" I ask. I'm taking advantage of the fact that he *has* to be nice to me right now, and you better believe I'm going to use that edge to keep him talking. Hopefully, this weekend I can disarm him enough that he can go back to being a nice guy—or at least not so hostile toward me.

"Well, there are over one hundred artists from twenty-two different countries, for one. People come from all over the world to meet their favorite tattoo artists. For another, I'm kind of a big deal—not that permanently marking people for a living elevates me as anything more than a common street rat in your eyes." He delivers his insult without even looking at me, which makes me think he wouldn't say it if he couldn't bestow it passive-aggressively.

"Can we be done with that yet? I was feeling manipulated by my friends and forced into something I didn't want to be a part of. It had nothing to do with you. As far as my callousness, I think that says more about me than it does about you. Ok? I'm an asshole. Can we please move on?" A few moments pass while he thinks about what I said, then he does look up at me.

"Fair enough. You're an asshole." This time there is nothing passive-aggressive about his demeanor, and he holds my eye contact until I'm the one that looks away.

Instead of continuing with this losing battle, I shift the focus back to him and his *kind of a big deal* ego. "How many tattoos do you think you'll end up doing tonight?" I ask, before I decide to arrange the hats differently and get to work on a different merchandise layout.

"I know exactly how many tonight—one. Two tomorrow, and two on Sunday."

"Why did I need to learn the scheduling software then?" At this point, I'm just trying to keep him talking. I don't give a rat's ass if I schedule appointments or not.

"The five people I have scheduled for this convention made their appointments between six and nine months ago, and they are paying a premium rate. No one expects to get in to see me this weekend. New appointments are for next year." He tears off the edge of the plastic and then sits down on his stool to begin wrapping everything else in barrier film.

"Oh, that reminds me, I made you a cheat sheet, so you know how much time to block out based on the size of the piece and how much of a deposit to collect. It's under the laptop."

"Got it."

"Since you are not sterilizing anything, you can head out around nine or ten. Just cover up the merchandise before you go. I'll clean everything up when I finish tattooing. Doors open at 11:00 tomorrow, but your vendor's wristband will get you in as early as 10:00."

"Ok."

"Are you staying close by?" he asks, and when I don't immediately answer, he looks up and meets my eyes. We've been so busy setting up that I haven't had any time to continue searching for a hotel room. I'd like to say I am not even considering staying at the bartender's house—because I'm really not, but what if?

"I'm not sure how close he lives to be honest." I try to keep my face from falling with the reminder of my situation because Gavin is still looking at me, and now he has stopped wrapping altogether.

"*What did you just say?*" he asks incredulously. I feel reprimanded by those five words, and it makes my spine straighten for battle. He doesn't get to treat me like crap *and* scold me like a child.

"*I said*, I don't know how close he lives. Now, do you want my help with the banner or not?"

"You let that bartender pick you up, didn't you?" He says it like it tastes dirty in his mouth, and he wants to spit it out.

"He didn't *pick me up!* He offered me a place to stay, so settle down—You don't need to concern yourself with my plans, anyway,

Gavin!" I shout. It came out harsher than I intended, but my accommodations are a sore spot, and he is poking the bruise.

"Are you insane? You are not staying with him! You only need *one* brain cell to know that's a bad idea. *Jesus, Alabama*—Please tell me you have **one** brain cell."

I don't answer him, partly because I have nothing intelligent to say—having zero brain cells and all, and partly because I might start crying if I stay here. He's right. It's stupid even to consider staying with a complete stranger.

The hotel is only three blocks away, so I exit the booth and blaze a trail in that direction. The prevailing emotion I carry with me is humiliation, so when I fish my phone out of my pocket, it's not to keep searching for a hotel room. It's to book a flight home.

"Alabama!" Gavin yells after me. By now, I'm on the crowded sidewalk and beelining straight to the hotel to get my suitcase. He is about to catch up with me, so I have roughly two seconds to dry my eyes and compose myself.

When he catches up, he doesn't grab me or spin me around. He steps right in my path and holds his ground. "I'm sorry." He says it like it's a lit explosive instead of an olive branch. I try to step around him, but he moves to the side as well.

It's not worth staying here to help him. It will cost me thousands of dollars to get a place or put me in danger at a random bartender's house—neither of which he deserves from me. I tried to rectify my initial nastiness, but now I'll just have to sit with it. There is no redeeming myself to him, and I'm done trying.

I step to the other side, so does he. I'm trying to summon my rage but in reality, I'm about to cry. Not just about how he speaks to me or my hotel room situation, but because I may have lost a whale of an account to be here, a last-minute flight home will cost a fortune, and I look like an idiot when all I was trying to do was leave him with a better impression of me.

"Alabama?" Now he does grab my arms, and the shock of his insistence tries to ignite a little fury again, but the squeak in my voice erases any of my indignation.

"What?" The word comes out exactly how I feel, deflated.

"You are not staying with some random dude. I'm surprised I have to tell you that." I need to rapid-blink to void the tears before I look up at him.

"You're right about that. I'm going ho—"

"You can stay in my room," he blurts out. The offer comes out like he is donating a kidney instead of offering his accommodations.

"I don't want to stay there." My words are finally strong because I can feel my desire to be away from him in every cell of my body.

"You don't always get what you want. I'll make some calls and find somewhere to stay; I've got buddies out here." Before I even have a chance to decline, he continues, "But you have to let me shower there today because we only have about ninety minutes to eat and get ready…and the banner is still not up."

I want to say no. I want to tell him he is on his own and that he's the real asshole, but what comes out instead is, "I'll eat at the hotel restaurant while you shower. Then I'll get ready and meet you over there."

***

Sam is no longer by himself behind the bar, and the restaurant is no longer empty. I order a Thai noodle bowl and sit, wondering why I couldn't have thought quicker on my feet. I should be headed to the airport, not about to shower in Gavin's room and be his mistreated personal assistant for the duration of the convention.

I hope Sam couldn't read the relief on my face when I told him there was a cancelation and I had a room at the hotel after all. A look of disappointment flashed across his face for a millisecond before he replaced it with a smile.

When he found out I'm working the tattoo convention tonight, he made me the most delicious *and strongest* coffee drink I've ever tasted. He is a genuinely nice guy, but I'd also like to think I would have paid for an overpriced room before following him home.

"Here comes, guns," he says as he wipes the bar in front of me and then points to the coffee, wondering if I would like another. When I turn toward Gavin, I suck in a sharp inhale that may have something to do with the amperage of my coffee drink.

He is wearing black pants, a pressed white shirt, and suspenders. He is also clean-shaven, but the part that makes my caffeine-addled heart beat double-time is that he combed back his hair. Now it's all stylish and trendy to go with the closely shorn sides of his head. He looks like he belongs in a vintage bourbon ad.

He walks over, spares a curt nod for Sam, and then slides the key card over to me by way of the highly lacquered bar top. Apparently, it's my cue to take my turn in the room. *Damn*, he smells good too—like a clean, masculine scented candle. His scent wafts lightly into my nostrils and probably blows out my pupils as it vasodilates every blood vessel in my body.

"Room 1017. I'll see you over there," he says as I watch the pulse in his neck thrum.

When he's gone, Sam raises an eyebrow at me that I pretend not to notice. Each of them seems a little territorial in their own way, but considering the shaky ground I'm on with each of them, I want nothing to do with their dick posturing. I pay, and over-tip Sam just because he is such a nice guy and then head off to Gavin's room.

***

If platinum had a warm, sexy scent that made me pinch my thighs together—that's what Gavin's room smells like. I don't know what that cologne is, but it acts like a pheromone on steroids inside my brain.

There is still a part of me that resists my growing attraction to him, and not because he barely tolerates me, but because he is so rough-around-the-edges. The thing is, though, even if he is not my type, he still has mountains of something intensely provocative.

Gavin's stuff is neatly tucked into the corner by the front door, obviously ready to run for the hills as soon as he nails down a new place to stay. If it weren't for that and his lingering essence that threatens to pry my legs apart, you'd never know he had been in here at all.

The room is beautiful but also very streamlined in a swanky, boutique hotel kind of way. There is not much more than a bed and a skinny desk that moonlights as a dresser as well. Even the nightstand is no more than a floating shelf, hardly big enough to fit a cell phone next to the lamp and clock. The TV looks like a framed piece of art, set to a melty looking abstract screensaver. That's it. Not even a chair to impede the wall of window glass covered by a sheer, white curtain.

The bed looks like an inviting cloud of queen-sized nirvana, except that it has probably ten different decorative pillows that I want to sweep to the floor due to the communal use, and grossness of them. The only time I'm a germaphobe in any capacity is when I'm in a hotel room, and stuff like deco pillows and community down comforters that are simply covered in a sheet is just, well…nasty.

I have less than an hour before I need to be at the convention, so I need to get in the shower. Gavin clearly went to some extra effort to look good, and I intend to do the same thing.

I open my suitcase to pick out some clothes. I always like to hang them in the steamy bathroom while I shower, so they look less like I've pulled them from the bowels of an airplane.

The first thing I notice is that Miles has left his mark. That sneaky fucker unpacked everything I had in here and re-packed according to his own agenda. What's worse, is that he also left me a note to further punctuate his packing supremacy.

You're welcome.

Chapter 11

In a different place, I would feel sexy dressed like this, but at a tattoo convention, I feel like an overdressed poser…without any tattoos. Thanks to Miles' devious nature, I am wearing a black pencil skirt that hits right below my knees, four-inch black heels, and a white strapless corset that's not really a corset because it is made out of cotton dress shirt material.

I went ahead and put beachy waves in my hair and left it down even though the ponytail holder was calling to me like an old friend. My makeup is done—not as heavy as Miles would have liked, and not with the false eyelashes he all but reached through the mirror to apply for me, but it's definitely more makeup than I usually wear.

The doors are not yet open, but the crowd already swells with a life and breath of its own. I feel like a supermodel strutting down the runway, but not a graceful, confident one. No, I feel like the one in wobbly platform shoes that's hardly holding it together and about to eat shit on the catwalk.

I get some leering looks, and I get some friendly smiles, but mostly I'm worried that the heads I'm turning are because of the neon sign above my head that flashes, *Outsider-Outsider-Outsider.* My vendor wristband gets me through the heavy doors with no more than a nod and a smile, and then I enter the vast event center that is brimming with possibilities.

For the most part, there are rows and rows of booths similar to Gavin's, but in the back of the convention hall is a giant, raised stage. It has enough metal scaffolding, rigging, and lighting for a Broadway production. At the moment, on the stage is a tiny slip of a woman in a flesh-colored bikini who looks to be preparing for a show.

Within moments, the type of show becomes clear because another woman—strikingly beautiful, with a long shimmering fall of hair that looks like a champion horse's tail, begins attaching hooks to the first woman's back. I stop in my tracks, wondering if *this* is the suspension show the marketing pamphlets and posters have been advertising.

I'm torn between watching this fiery train wreck and continuing on toward Gavin's booth. *She is going to hang from the hooks in her back!* I'm frozen in place until the fleshy peaks that line her back begin to pull further away from her body, then I've seen enough—and her feet aren't even off the ground yet.

When I get close to our booth, I slow my approach, so I don't look too eager, or like I'm running from a couple of fleshy meat-hooks. Gavin looks over and smiles brightly before his eyes and brain connect the fact that it's *me* he is smiling at. Then, like warm butter, his smile melts right off his face.

"I wasn't sure if you would get here in time, so I already got Joel's paperwork together. It's next to the laptop. He'll be here any minute. He's already texted me twice." He talks while buzzing around like a busy worker bee, making sure the lighting is right and that everything is wrapped in plastic and laid out where he wants it on the tray.

"Ok," I say. I'm feeling even less confident about how I'm dressed after seeing his smile dissolve and be replaced with pure indifference. I hoped to see a reaction similar to the one I had after seeing him all put together. I guess there is not enough makeup and tight clothing in all of LA to get his attention the way he got mine.

"I'm a little worried about time, so I need to get started right away. It's a big piece, and I only have seven hours." Now, Gavin has given me his back and could be speaking to the wall for all he's concerned.

"So, what are you doing on him?" I ask, as breezily as I can while I casually look around the space. He must have had someone else help him with the banner because it's up—and somehow, loud and dominating.

"Alabama," he says, sounding disappointed, "We've been over this a thousand times. I'm doing a *tattoo* on him." Then he smiles, but I'm not sure if he means it for me or for the guy that has just charged into our airspace from behind me. It must be his client because they are doing the man-hug thing and suddenly talking like long-lost brothers.

"Who's your friend?" the guy asks as he slaps Gavin's shoulder in camaraderie. He has a full beard but a bald head, which conflicts with nature a bit for me. His earlobes are stretched out big enough to fit a quarter, but for now, they just hang empty and limp. He is also as fit as they come. What I can't figure out is where Gavin would put a tattoo on him because he appears to be completely covered—from his jawline to his ripped, calf-length pants and combat boots.

"This is, Alabama," Gavin offers, bored already with the shift in conversation.

The man steps toward me and says, "Hello, Alabama. I'm Phillip. It's nice to meet you." As he speaks, his eyes slowly troll up my body, from my ankles to my eyes. I start to hand him the clipboard, but he scoffs and crosses his arms over his chest. Apparently, arrogance travels in pairs.

"Phillip and I have tattooed in the same circles for years," Gavin explains. "You won't find a better Neo-Traditional tattoo artist." Then Gavin shifts his focus and talks to Phillip again, "What are you working on this weekend?"

"Sternum tonight." They both wince, and I take careful note never to get my sternum tattooed. "Finishing up a back piece tomorrow, maybe some quick flash. Depends on time." I leave them to their little bromance because now the client really is here, and I want to get him started on all the paperwork.

The doors must finally open because the crowd comes in like high tide. There is a scramble of initial chaos, and while Joel does paperwork, Gavin greets the masses and signs autographs, and I try to keep up with people buying prints and t-shirts to have Gavin sign.

Things settle down once Gavin has Joel on the table, and his feet are no longer available for the commoners to anoint. He told me that people come from all over to have him do their tattoos because he is so well known for his portraiture work. He also said he is kind of a big deal—which at the time I took for his galactic sized ego, but it turns out he might be kind of a big deal.

For a while, I busy myself with selling and restocking merchandise, but no one wants to talk to me or make any appointments. So the best I can do is keep filling his business card holder and continue to keep the product display table looking organized. People stop to watch Gavin work, but they don't ask him a lot of questions because they respect that he is working. I try to stay out of his hair as well because he warned me, in no uncertain terms, to keep out of his sterile field.

He has the photo of a child taped to the edge of his surgical tray, and he periodically glances at it. So far, nothing has really taken shape, but it's only been like…an hour. How he manages to create something that resembles a person from the purple chaos of his stencil, I will never understand. It's just as well. He isn't interested in getting to know anything about me, so trying to figure out all his little nuances is pretty pointless.

As if sensing my boredom, Gavin glances up at me. "You can go check things out if you want to. It's a big convention."

"Ok," my back is to him practically before he even finished setting me free. The crowd swallows me whole. It consists of everyone from young families with kids in strollers to grizzled old men and everyone in between.

There are a ton of talented artists here, most of them selling their own brand of merchandise and many of them posing for pictures and rubbing elbows with starstruck fans.

After a while, I don't feel out of place anymore. This is partly due to the fact that there is every walk of life here and partly because a decent percentage of women wear retro attire. It's like they've channeled their inner Vargas Girl. They wear Pin-up style shorts and tops, high-waisted capri pants, and vintage swing dresses. Thanks to Miles, I fit in nicely—and no one is more surprised about that fact than me.

There is so much going on and *so* much to see as I wander around. The first presentation platform that catches my eye is a body modification demonstration, and it holds my rapt attention for over an hour. The whole thing is utterly captivating, and he presents it like a scholarly seminar.

The modifications are shown on a large flat-screen TV, while the expert alternates between standing behind a podium and pacing the platform like a lecturing college professor.

By the time I walk away, I'm entirely too knowledgeable about tongue splitting and subdermal implants, but the whole presentation was oddly fascinating. I'm sure my jaw hung open for at least a third of the presentation.

I've spent my whole life being forced into a mold, and taught that anything outside of those very specific parameters was unacceptable or worse, deviant. It would have been nice to learn from a young age that there are all kinds of people in the world. All of them acceptable, and the vast majority of them having nothing to do with me.

I think such realizations would have served me well and broadened my character. To hell with what such an upbringing would have meant to my father's career.

I don't abide by ignorant societal labels when it comes to the people I choose to be around. Would I like Miles more if he dated women? Absolutely not. Would Ivy be more important to me if her skin was white? God, no. Would I prefer it if Arden didn't date a police officer? No.

In fact, I'm starting to wonder if Gavin may be the same life lesson for me, but this time wrapped in tattoos. Maybe I haven't learned the skill of not judging others from a keyhole view clearly enough. So, karma sent it back around to see if I can grasp it with both hands this time.

It's not enough to be in the trenches with Miles and Ivy in their battles with homophobia and racism. And truly, nothing gets my hackles up faster than hearing the derogatory terms hurled at Miles, or seeing the sideways looks Ivy gets when she dates a white guy. Or any of the other thousands of ways the world tries to deny them or spit them out for not being a certain way.

The universe must be wondering where all my righteous convictions are now, seeing that they didn't initially extend to the tattooed. It appears that fate's rotating wheel intends to stop for a bit to rub my nose in my harbored prejudices for a little while. The universe is laughing too, because teaching me that Gavin *is* a great catch is poetic justice in its purest form.

As I look around, I see kids everywhere—beautiful, unique kids, all experiencing life through a broad-spectrum approach. I'd like to say I will raise my kids the same way, especially because of how my own upbringing has hobbled me, but in all honesty, I'd still have a stroke if my kid came home with a forked tongue or devil horn subdermal implants in his forehead.

As I make my way to the main stage at the back of the convention hall, I can see a fashion show going on. Actually, calling it a fashion show might be kind of a stretch because these models are hardly dressed. The production before me is more about them showcasing their prodigious amount of ink.

"Are you having a good time?" the man standing next to me asks. He's probably a few years older than me and very good-looking. He also has a hoop that hugs the middle of his bottom lip, so it's hard not to stare at it. He notices, and his smile broadens.

"I am. There is so much to see, I had no idea," I say, sounding more awestruck than I'm entirely comfortable with.

"Have you ever seen the SuicideGirls?" he leans closer to speak even though I can hear him just fine.

"I'm sorry...what did you say?" I ask. Talking about suicide seems like a quantum leap from whether or not I'm having a good time.

"The burlesque show, the SuicideGirls. Have you ever seen them perform before?"

"Oh. No, I haven't," I can't think of anything else to say because his proximity is getting closer, and he has a mischievous glint in his eye. I think he is flirting but isn't any good at it. It's like he has always relied on his looks to drop panties and never mastered the skill verbally.

"Let's go have dinner, and we can come back for the show at 9:30 when there is more of an adult crowd. The performance is incredibly sexy. I'd love for you to see it."

I can't help but feel like this guy is going to have sex with a few different women this weekend. He gives off the vibe of someone who constantly swipes right just to see who floats to the top. Maybe I'm wrong, but that's what I'm picking up from him.

"Actually, I'm supposed to be working," I tell him, but the truth is, it might do me some good to have someone look at me the way he is. It's like he wants to dive down between my legs and never come up for air.

"Oh, yeah? You have a booth?" He licks his tongue across his bottom lip and then purposely toys with the piercing for an extra second or two.

"Not me, no. I'm here with Gavin Rhodes," I say.

His eyes widen a fraction, and he backs up a half-step. He looks less lust-drunk now and has straightened his spine in a more regimented stance. It's like he all of a sudden realized that I smell like burnt hair. It's a strange reaction.

"Make sure you catch the SuicideGirls. You won't be disappointed," he says, and with that, he nods formally and then backs away into the masses.

***

When I return to the booth, Gavin is in much the same position that I left him in, and that was hours ago. The hot lights above him are making their presence felt in the form of tiny beads of sweat on his forehead. It gives me the urge to delicately swipe them away with my fingers.

When he finally looks up and acknowledges me, I ask, "Lemonade or iced tea?" I wasn't sure if he needed caffeine or wanted to avoid the stimulant in favor of a steady hand, so I brought options.

He slides his stool back, "Lemonade would be amazing." Then he puts his equipment down on the Chucks covered surgical tray and removes his gloves in two succinct movements. He wipes his forehead with the back of his wrist and then takes the drink from me.

"Thank you."

I didn't think he could take a break, or I would have brought him something to eat too. The concession stands and food trucks offer everything from street tacos to snow cones, and there are several micro-breweries in attendance as well. I myself, have slapped a face-sized funnel cake to my ass and thighs and had a pint of something dark and viscous.

He sucks down the lemonade, tosses the cup in the trash, squirts some hand sanitizer on his hands, then grabs two more latex gloves from the box. He is very dedicated to his work, even though it requires him to sit hunched over for hours on end. I'm too squirrelly for that. You'd have to lock me in an Iron Maiden to keep me still for seven hours.

I come as close as I dare. This time when I glance at his work, even from over here, I can tell it's a little girl's face. He's really good because her pouty lips look juicy and moist, and I can see each individual strand of hair in her curls. I don't know how he managed it with needles, but the child is brightly lit from the side, just like in the photo. The way he has shadowed the tattoo brings life to her face that almost giggles.

"How is it looking?" the client, Joel asks. I think he is talking to me, so, I answer.

"She looks beautiful. Really, it's astonishing how real she looks." Joel smiles wistfully and then closes his eyes, falling back into his trance.

When 9:25 rolls around, I feel a slight pull toward the main stage, but duty keeps me inserting credit cards into the chip reader on Gavin's phone. Tomorrow, I will plan my excursions away from the booth better. I looked at the main stage schedule for Saturday and Sunday, and there are aerial performers, cabaret shows, contortionists, bands, and more performances by the SuicideGirls. However, by all accounts, the not to be missed show is the pyro/aerial performance by the Fuel Girls.

As for tonight, the convention closes at 11:00, but Gavin is racing to finish his tattoo by 10:15 because Joel already entered it in a few contests, and the judging begins promptly at 10:30. Joel had to have entered the contests before Gavin even punctured his skin, so I'm assuming his confidence in Gavin's ability is fairly resolute.

He finishes in plenty of time, and while Joel and I ogle the finished product, Gavin cleans the freshly-inked area then opens a single-use packet of ointment and applies it gently.

"After judging, come back here, and I'll bandage it for you. By law, you need to have it covered when you leave." Gavin snaps off his gloves and then walks over to pull up the invoice on his laptop. "You can pay Alabama," he says as he sanitizes his hands again before announcing, "I have to pee like a racehorse." Then he disappears into the tattooed throngs of what's left of the crowd.

I choke on my surprise as I look over the invoice. There is a credit for his deposit in the amount of $500, and the total is *still* $3,000. Joel is unfazed by the number and adds a $600 tip to boot. It's insane, that's almost $600 dollars an hour!

When Gavin returns from the restroom, he asks me to go to the stage where they judge the tattoos while he cleans up. I'm surprised he doesn't want my help, so I pause.

"If Joel's tattoo wins, I'll need to be there for the awards and photos, but I want to get this all cleaned up so we can get out of here." Then he takes a deep breath and simplifies things for me, "Just come get me if he wins." He has already re-gloved and is taking his machine apart when I turn and follow Joel in the direction of the contest judging.

When they announce Joel as a finalist for the Best Black and Gray Tattoo, I run back to the booth as fast as my high heels and pencil skirt will allow me to. The convention-goers have dwindled significantly, so the process is a lot smoother than it would have been an hour ago.

Gavin looks annoyed when I summon him and asks, "What's this one for?" as he pulls off his gloves and gets ready to follow me.

"Best Black and Gray," I say. Is it possible I am more excited than him? When we arrive at the stage, they are handing a plaque to the winner and another one to the grinning artist. A handful of onlookers with press passes are allowed onto the platform and start snapping photos like bona fide paparazzi.

It's hard to read Gavin's reaction to losing because all he says is, "I'm fucking starving," and then heads back to the booth.

Joel looks astonished his tattoo didn't win and finds me as soon as he steps down from the stage. "That was some stiff competition, huh?"

"Yeah, it was. Gavin didn't seem to care, though," I say, surprised because even *I* am disappointed. That tattoo looks *exactly* like the photo Joel is still holding in his hand. It is shockingly perfect. So much so, that if that tattoo stood up and started singing Hallelujah—I wouldn't even be surprised. Gavin was robbed.

In the end, I needn't have been so indignant because Gavin won *Best Tattoo of the Day*. I was proud of him as I watched him accept his plaque and pose for all the photos. When he looked over at me between camera flashes, he caught me with my hands clasped together in front of my mouth and a dewy look in my eyes.

After descending the stairs and being accosted by a couple of fans—whom he politely conversed with for at least ten minutes—he comes over to where I'm standing.

"Want to go celebrate your win?" I ask. I want to throw my arms around his neck and congratulate him, but we are far from being on those familiar terms.

"Only if celebrating means eating a bacon cheeseburger," he says, and with that comment, I feel like we have fallen right back into our roles of cautious enemies. He acts like I'm the last person he would ever want to celebrate with. Well, at least his grumpy façade is back in place.

I can't think of how to respond to his snub, so I turn around and head back to the booth to retrieve my purse and phone. I'd like to be on the phone while I walk back to the hotel, even if it is only a few blocks, I will feel safer.

Once I fish my phone out of my purse, Gavin stuns me by saying, "Give me ten minutes, and we can go find something close by." It's almost as if he really had accepted my offer to go out and celebrate. He runs so hot and cold, I don't bother trying to unravel his meaning. I just sit on his stool and watch while he removes parts of his tattoo machine from the Ultrasonic cleaning unit, scrubs them in some sort of solution, slides each piece into a special sterilization pack, and then seals them up. He writes something on each bag before placing them in the Autoclave and turning it on.

"Ready to go?" he asks as he shoves his hands into his pockets and looks at me expectantly.

"Yep. Do you mind if we swing by the hotel first, though? That, or these heels are headed into the nearest trash can because my feet are killing me."

"We can't have that now, can we?" he says, and as usual I have trouble deciphering his meaning. Does he mean, he can't have me throw away these ridiculously sexy shoes? Or does he mean, we can't allow my delicate, princess feet to hurt? Never mind—of course, it's the latter.

Chapter 12

After making a quick stop at the hotel for me to change into the most sensible shoes Miles allowed to make the trip—which are still not all that sensible, I decided my pencil skirt had worn out its welcome as well and put on jeans instead. When I emerge from the elevator, Gavin is waiting stiffly in the lobby—probably seething mad that I managed to commandeer his room. As far as I'm concerned, he deserves to sleep on a buddy's couch this weekend because he still hasn't shown me an ounce of gratitude for being here at all. Anyway, now we are off to Gavin's chosen bacon cheeseburger venue.

***

I think the entire event center emptied out into this very bar. The venue is ridiculously packed despite its limited square footage. There is also a layer of sweat in the air and a live band playing country music on the stage.

Gavin parts the crowd like the Red Sea, apparently with his greatness alone—which does nothing except fold me into the swarm of revelers. I'm not interested in beating everyone back to retain my spot by his side, so I head straight for the bar and the strongest drink I can summon.

After two quick shots of something horrific, I'm a little surprised to see a familiar face. Once I make my way over to her, she shocks me by doling out a surprisingly tight hug for someone I've only known for three hours.

"Hi, Alabama! I'm so glad you are here. Did you give any more thought to coming to see me tomorrow?" When she asks this, I'm not sure if she means, do I plan on keeping her company at her booth again, or do I plan to let her shove needles through my body. She saves me the trouble of an answer when she yells, "I love this song!" Then grabs me by my hand and beats her own path through all the people.

Her name is Sunrise, which is easy for me to remember because I think she is the only person alive that can pull off that name. That and, if a sunrise had a personality, it would be her. She is spunky and gorgeous, and I think the brilliant smile on her face was born there and has remained in place her whole life.

I met Sunrise earlier tonight when I stopped at her booth to watch her pierce a guy's septum. Nothing out of the ordinary happened until the guy's girlfriend grabbed my arm and announced that she wanted ear piercings just like mine. She stunned me enough by snatching my arm, that I allowed her to tow me over to Sunrise as her living example.

I figured I was invested enough at that point to hang around while the girlfriend had three holes punched through her ear, and then stayed another hour just chatting with Sunrise. If it were possible to be both a bolt of lightning and a ray of sunshine, that would be her, and her personality drew me in completely.

"I love this song, but I don't know the dance. Do you think they will care if I go out there anyway?" she asks. She may be nervous about dancing with this group, but in no way is it enough to stop her.

"Sunrise, this is the Electric Slide, and it will take you four and a half minutes to learn. Come on." Now it's my turn to drag her to the dance floor. I haven't line danced since college, and if you told me a week ago that I'd be country dancing in a Los Angeles bar right now, I would have told you to put down the crack pipe.

As far as the line dance goes, Sunrise picks it up pretty quickly, and before long, I have a small group of eager learners clustered around me. One such learner is an elderly man wearing a Vietnam War Veteran hat, which puts him at an age where dancing in an LA bar elevates him to rock-star status.

I'm only vaguely aware of Gavin's presence at the bar, but I can feel it like an itch down the back of my neck. When I catch him looking at me, I've got my arm around the Vietnam Vet's waist, and I've slowed down the steps to help him learn them easier. I'm so flustered Gavin caught me glancing at him that I flub the next couple of moves, and it takes me a few seconds to re-focus my nervous energy.

After a handful of songs, I feel like the stress from this morning has mostly dissipated, and I feel relaxed yet amped up. I've quickly settled into having a lot of fun dancing with my protégés—that, or the caffeine jolt from Sam's earlier coffee drink has hit me like the stray crack of a whip.

At one point, the lead singer of the band gestured me over, and when I stepped forward, he put his cowboy hat on my head. I think he felt it necessary for me to wear one while line dancing to Cotton-Eyed Joe. However, putting a cowboy hat, heated by another, onto my own sweaty head only served to raise my temperature a solid ten degrees.

By the time Sunrise and I have danced so much, we've shed ten pounds of water weight, the bar has emptied out quite a bit. At the same time, Gavin's fan club has dwindled to a few guys, including his Neo-Traditional tattoo buddy that I met earlier today.

While I'm wondering if one of the guys standing next to him is also the friend he's staying with, I feel a tap on my shoulder.

"May I have this dance?"

This actually marks the first time someone has ever asked me to dance with them. The fact that he wants my humid existence anywhere near him is equally as surprising. And because the giant teddy bear of a man has such a nervous, worried look on his face, I decide to dance with him.

"Of course," I say as I place one hand on his upper arm and the other in his hand. My last two-step partner was Ivy, and this guy is twice her size and triple her weight. I feel like I'm dancing with a brick wall.

The poor guy was so timid when he asked, and the fact that he fully expected to be rejected made me want to dance with him. This might help him have a tiny bit more confidence the next time he approaches a woman.

As we make our way around the dance floor, I see Gavin *and* his two buddies looking at us. Which all but confirms they are talking about me. Gavin's face is unreadable, but the other two guys are smiling like Jackals. Their fixed attention makes this cowboy hat feel even more like a furnace on top of my head.

When the song is over, I tell the guy he is a great partner and thank him for asking me to dance with him. I overdo it, but I'm seriously hoping it helps him not be so nervous next time he talks to a girl.

I get Sunrise's attention to let her know I'm going to get some water from the bar. Then, as I'm handing the cowboy hat back to the singer, he surprises me by hopping off the stage and holding out his hand. It looks like I'm two-stepping again.

The band carries on fine without him, but when he quietly sings the song just to me while spinning me around the dance floor, I giggle. The giggle is purely out of discomfort, though, because it's weird to have a stranger looking into my eyes and singing to me. If I had known wearing his hat branded me in some way, I would have skipped it.

"What's your name, pretty girl?" he asks.

"Alabama." I'm so uncomfortable I don't even ask for his name. The first guy was nothing but a gentleman, even after he loosened up while talking and dancing. This guy is the opposite. He wants to take me backstage and introduce me to his zipper.

"Stay and have a drink with me tonight, Alabama."

"Oh. Um. Thank you, but my boyfriend is waiting for me at the bar." I awkwardly put the hat back on his head, and he backs up before spinning me under his arm one last time as the song ends. I loathe the fact that Gavin and his friends saw me get passed around like germs in preschool—and I know they did because the crowd has dwindled so much.

I'm not sure what protocol is right now. I'm ready to leave, but since Gavin isn't staying in the hotel, and I haven't hung out with him all night, I'm not sure if I should tell him I'm leaving. Do I say goodbye? Do I wave?

I finally decide to at least tell him that I'll see him tomorrow, but as I make my way over to them, I almost lose my nerve. They all watch me approach, and I have no idea what any of them are thinking.

"Looks like your dance card is pretty full tonight, hot stuff," Gavin says with a sneer before raising his beer bottle to his lips.

Before I can respond—or even flush with embarrassment, the band launches into a particularly rousing version of *Sweet Home Alabama*, and the three guys in front of me dissolve with laughter.

I look right at Phillip, the Neo-Traditional tattoo phenom who also happens to be the most heavily tattooed of the three of them.

"Laugh it up, Phillip—I told him you were my boyfriend," I say with raised eyebrows and a squared-off jaw. Gavin and the other guy laugh, but Phillip sucks in his breath—right before his lips slide into a devious looking grin.

"Is that right?" he asks, with one eye on Gavin and one on me. "Then, I do believe your last dance is reserved for me," he delivers his words slowly and methodically as his eyebrows rise up his forehead.

"You even know how to dance, Dawg?" the other guy asks as he shifts the chewed-on toothpick in his mouth to the other side.

"Are you kidding me? I grew up in Wyoming—I'll own that dancefloor." Then he places his hand on my lower back and says, "Let's dance, *Lover*."

As we approach the dance floor, the band abruptly stops playing Sweet Home Alabama, and they begin a very upbeat Shania Twain song. It looks like my tribute song is over, but they don't want to risk playing a slow song either. I look over at Phillip, unsure how he is taking the shift in tempo.

"Don't worry, baby girl, I got this," he says as he winks and joins in on the initial *stomp, stomp, clap* that the song seems to require. When he gets the subsequent toe and heel taps right, it's obvious he knows what he's doing. Unfortunately, I'm a little rusty on this one, so I spend a good amount of the song laughing at myself and remaining a half step behind everyone else.

I have to be honest though, part of what is so funny to me is Phillip. He is all tatted up—wearing combat boots and a wallet chain, but despite how out of place he looks, he *is* owning the floor—just like he said he would. He's good, and his huge grin is completely charming. He even adds in all the fancy, extra dance moves just to show everyone else up.

Between you and me, I think he is relishing the fact that he is so unexpected. Just being able to disprove his stereotype and obliterate everyone's assumptions about him must feel really good. Tattoos or not—this guy can country dance.

We stay on the floor for the next handful of songs, and I've got to be honest, I haven't laughed this hard or had this much fun in a very long time. I am really starting to enjoy my first tattoo convention. Who would have thought?

After another song change—upbeat of course, Phillip decides on his own to turn it into a slow dance. He leads me to the perimeter of the floor and dances me around the small group of newly impressed dancers.

"You sure you and Gavin are just friends?" he asks as he weaves me around everyone like a pro. I haven't told him that, so evidently, Gavin has. That's probably better than the truth, though.

"I'm not too sure we are even *friends*. He barely tolerates me, and the only reason I'm here is because his employee canceled at the last minute."

"Girl, you're talking nonsense. What makes you think that's all you are to him?"

"I dunno, maybe *everything* that comes out of his mouth," I emphasize.

"Does he look like a crazy man to you?"

"Often, yes."

Phillip clicks his tongue, "I've known that man a long time, and I've never known him to be crazy. I've also never seen him look at anyone the way he looks at you." This last statement stops me in my tracks.

"I think you might be misinterpreting that look."

He hauls me back into step with him, "And you may be misinterpreting *everything that comes out of his mouth*." I think about Phillip's words for a tender second before I remember Gavin calling me *a cunt*, and the tenderness dissolves.

"Hey, can I get in on this?" Sunrise says from behind me. Her timing could not be more perfect because I don't know how to respond to Phillip, and my feet are ready to be out of these shoes and in bed.

"Sure. Come here, my little ray of sunshine," Phillip releases me with hardly a second thought, and the two of them fuse together. They have clearly met before because the energy that crackles all around them reads *unrequited love.*

Gavin intercepts me as I walk off the dance floor and asks, "You ready to go?" I'm surprised by his question because we have separate destinations. Still, it makes me happy that he cares about me getting back safely.

"Yeah, let's go."

Chapter 13

As Gavin and I walk the few blocks back to the hotel, he seems especially quiet and uncomfortable. Everything becomes clear when he finally opens his mouth.

"Alabama, we are going to have to share the room tonight." I stop walking while he continues, "I didn't want to tell you sooner because it's really not safe for you to stay at that bartender's place. I *know* I won't touch you, but I can't say the same for him."

I pause with his comment. *I **know** I won't touch you*—it sort of feels like a machete to the self-esteem after letting Phillip's words from earlier start to marinate.

I still haven't resumed walking, and I've been stunned into silence. The first thing I think about is the bed because it's not even king-sized. And the second thing I think about is the fact that I don't have anything to sleep in except the slutty scrap of see-through mesh that Miles packed. I can't even remedy that right now because it's almost two in the morning and nothing is open.

"I'm serious, you don't have to worry about me trying anyth—"

"I get it, ok?" God-damn, he doesn't need to rub it in.

"I'll even sleep on the floor."

"*Awesome.*"

***

When we get back to the room, it's beyond awkward. To be honest, my feelings are still a little stung that he was so revolted by the thought of touching me. I hadn't even thought that far ahead, and he was already assuring me that he'd rather chew his own arm off than brush up against me in a shared bed.

When he pulls the extra blanket and pillow out of the closet and begins setting up his makeshift bed on the floor, he looks really handsome. He has untucked his shirt, and his suspenders are hanging in discarded loops from his waist.

"Gavin, we are both adults. You can sleep in the bed too." He looks at me as if to gauge my seriousness, and then nods his head but doesn't say anything.

"Can I ask you for a favor, though?" I mumble. There is no way I can wear any of my clothes to bed and not look like I'm trying to seduce him.

He stops what he is doing and braces both hands on his hips. The cocksure way he is standing, coupled with his styled hair and the rolled-up sleeves of his dress shirt, makes me want to go back in time. Just far enough to see if I could lick that tattoo off his neck instead of stressing how much he isn't my type.

I think his swagger alone makes him more my type than the last five guys I've dated. His arrogance too. Although I don't actually think he *is* arrogant—it's more of a panty-melting confidence mixed with an aura of greatness.

"Spit it out, Alabama."

"Right, do you have…I mean, did you happen to bring…uh—"

"Alabama, I'm fucking exhausted, get on with it."

"Do you happen to have an extra t-shirt?" I finally force out. The sly grin that splits his face is nothing short of lecherous, and his long pause makes me almost wish I was at the bartender's house right now.

"Nope, sure don't." The amusement is dripping from his smile as he slowly shakes his head back and forth.

"Um-kay." I literally have nothing to say right now, so I just stand here like a fool. "Well, I guess I'll go wash the sweat off me before bed. Do you need to use the bathroom first?"

"Hey, Alabama?"

"What?"

"Did you happen to bring any extra jammie bottoms for me?"

***

It's way too late to wash my hair right now, so I pile it on top of my head in a chaotic bun so it won't get wet in the shower. A quick bathroom inventory of my suitcase proves what I already know. The sundress I wore on the way here is too stiff and too tight to sleep in. The "pajamas" Miles packed for me is a see-through, plum colored, boner maker, and it would serve Gavin right if I wore it.

The problem is, I would crumble like Pompei ash if he laughed at me or was unimpressed in any way. I've also got thigh high stockings with a line up the back, a garter belt to go with them, a short pleated skirt, a leather halter top, tight black cigarette pants, a plunging top that I can't even wear a bra with, two lace bodysuits, a bralette, and enough skimpy bras and panties for a week. Fucking Miles. Nothing—and I mean *nothing* to sleep in.

I take an exorbitantly long shower and then spend fifteen minutes applying lotion just to ensure Gavin is asleep. I think—only slightly less ridiculous than sleeping in my pre-shower jeans and corset, would be wearing the bralette under the plum teddy to remedy the see-throughness of the top.

However, there is nothing to be done for the bottom. Every single one of the panties in my suitcase are stupid-sexy—the kind you never even wear unless you are trying to seduce someone, yeah, those.

When I finally come out of the bathroom, supremely humiliated in this ridiculous get-up, I see Gavin in bed. His back is to me, and he is blessedly asleep. And, I might add, as far over as he can be while still remaining on the bed. I also see a folded white t-shirt with a note on my side of the bed. It's dark in here, but with the light from the bathroom, I can still read it.

Will this work?

Oh, thank God! I grab the shirt and dash back into the bathroom to peel off the current stupidity. My excitement is short-lived though, because I realize it's not a t-shirt at all. It's a men's ribbed tank top. Of course my vintage-style tattoo artist roommate wears tanks instead of t-shirts. *Of course.*

It covers my ass just *barely* and leaves some gratuitous side-boob, but it will be fine as long as I get up first in the morning—which I will make sure I absolutely do.

I set my alarm for ten because the convention doesn't open until 11:00, and it's horrendously late right now. In fact, due to our early flight, I've now been up for over 24 hours.

Gavin had done exactly what everyone else does with those damn deco pillows—dumped them straight onto the dirty floor. So, now I guess there is nothing left to do except saddle up.

I slide into bed as gently as possible and pull the blanket up to my chin. *Jesus*—the bed smells like him. Even in my sleep, I won't be able to escape his looming sex appeal.

I wonder what he is wearing right now?

Was he kidding about not having jammie bottoms?

What if he is in bed naked—at this exact moment?

I hate this stupid, overstuffed pillow.

The pillow is so big—my head would be at a ninety-degree angle if I slept on it. It's a sorry excuse for a pillow. I'm a tummy sleeper, and my pillows at home are fluffy down and essentially flat—unless I squish them together. I think I'd rather have my own pillows from home than pajamas right now.

Chapter 14

When I wake up, I'm confused…and mortified. While sleeping on my stomach, I have scooched down the bed just enough to have my head essentially in Gavin's armpit, my arm thrown over his waist, and my face pressed against his side. His naked torso touching my nose and lips is shocking enough, but to make matters worse, the blanket bunches between my legs, so half of my ass is uncovered.

I'd like to say I use a certain amount of stealth when extracting myself from the situation so that I don't wake Gavin up, but that's not entirely true. In fact, that's not at all true. I sit up so fast that when I get to my knees and sit back on my heels, I have to scramble to bunch the covers in front of my non-panty-panties.

"Do you always start the day with this much fanfare?" he asks as he rolls onto his side to face me, supporting his sleepy stubble with his hand.

"I'm just. You know… So, hey—what time is it?" I'm trying hard to be nonchalant, but I'm sure he can *see* my heart pounding through his tank top. Luckily, my theatrics woke him up, so he wasn't aware of me nuzzled against his side. At least, that's what I tell myself.

"Almost ten." He gets out of bed *shirtless* and then stretches his arms toward the ceiling. The exaggerated stretch manages to ripple his abs and lower his waistband. Damn him and his disheveled hotness. Tattoos cover his arms, but the rest of his torso is bare—of ink and hair.

"That's some crazy hair you've got there, Alabama," he says as he rounds the foot of the bed in his low-slung sweatpants.

I have no words to respond to him. I thought he looked good yesterday all styled and polished, but the sight of him rumpled and scruffy from sleep actually dries out my throat.

"Do you need to use the bathroom before I get in the shower?" he asks with a foamy electric toothbrush in his mouth. The truth is, yes, I have to use the bathroom desperately, but I would rather pee in this bed than walk past him dressed like this. I'm not taking the sheet off my lower half until he gets under the spray of the shower.

He walks back into the bathroom and spits into the sink. "It's not like I didn't already see your lacy ass this morning," he says, coming into view once again. The toothbrush is back in his mouth while he shrugs with indifference.

That comment imparts the knowledge that he *did* see my uncovered ass this morning. Which also means he knows I woke up snuggled against him.

"Just hurry up," I say on a sigh. If it was possible for my words to blush with embarrassment, they would have.

As soon as he is in the shower, I spring out of bed and grab my clothes for the day. I don't have a ton of time to think about it, so I snatch the leather halter top and short pleated skirt. This is the outfit Miles had in mind for me to wear with the garter belt. It's really sexy because it will provide little peaks of the garter instead of an overtly showy announcement. After a few seconds of wicked contemplation, I decide to fight fire with fire, and add the thigh highs and garter belt to my bathroom pile.

If he is going to strut around here half-naked and flexing his perfect bod, well then, I'm going to have to try a little harder to get his attention. Two can play at this game. I *am* worried, however, that I won't play it nearly as well as he can, but I figure, I can't be afraid of the wind *and* sail.

I undo the pile of hair from the back of my head and shake it out—fortunately for me, my hair is always better on day two. I also want to get some makeup on before he's done in there, so I better speed it up.

When he does come out of the bathroom, it's in a swirl of steam like a sexy apparition, and he's wearing jeans, but nothing else. I try to remain unflustered as I apply lipstick in the full-length mirror, but there is no chance of that. His half-nakedness is too big of a personality—it takes up the entire room.

While he moves around the hotel room sprinkling his pheromones like pixie dust and leaving the scent of clean lumberjack in his wake, I go into the bathroom and pee what must be a ten-minute stream of held urine.

As I stand in the bathroom holding my toothbrush at the ready, I have to push back his words that keep bubbling to the surface of my consciousness—*You aren't my type either, I don't even like redheads.*

In case you think I haven't noticed the irony in this situation, let me assure you, I've noticed. And this particular dose of karmic justice tastes just like fat, greasy crow. I'm not sure if Gavin and I can ever move past our initial meeting, but I'm going to infuse a little of Miles' intention into everything I do from this point forward. I'm not much for big guns, but I can pull them out when absolutely necessary.

When Gavin leans against the bathroom door jamb to see if I'm ready yet, I lean over the counter a little more because I can't quite apply my mascara right unless I'm closer to the mirror—*and* bent over so he can see the dangling straps from the garter belt along with the backs of my bare thighs.

"You all.....set?" he asks, faltering the tiniest bit.

"Yep, I just need to get my stockings and shoes on." I breeze past him wondering if the faint scent of my lotion infiltrates his senses the same way his body wash does mine.

When I sit on the end of the bed to slide my thigh-highs on, Gavin remains in the bathroom, presumably to give me some privacy while fiddling with his grooming products and shaving cream.

I can't bring myself to wear the super high heels from yesterday, but the ones I choose are still very sexy because of the double strap around my ankles. They are only marginally more comfortable than the ones I wore yesterday, proving that Miles wasn't concerned with my comfort when he packed them.

"Hey, Gavin? Can you come give me a hand please?"

"What do you need? We are going to be late," he says as he makes eye contact with me, his annoyance firmly in place.

"Can you attach the backs of these? I can never get them on straight," my request comes as I turn around in front of him, knowing damn well he knows exactly what I'm talking about.

He exhales a gruff sigh and then squats down behind me. "I gotta be honest. I'm usually the one taking these things off—not putting them on." His words steal my breath as effectively as a punch in the chest, and when his hand grazes just a hint of skin above the lace, his touch sizzles a concise path straight to the nerve center in my brain. Or, more accurately, the nerve center in my pelvis.

When finished attaching the straps, he smacks my ass like a football coach telling me to *go get em, champ*. When I recover from that and turn around, he is holding the door open for me and appearing impatient. Looks like round one goes to *him*.

Chapter 15

If I based my tattoo convention knowledge on yesterday, then I clearly need to readjust my expectations because today is like day one—with an exponent of five. The insanity of trying to keep up with everyone's purchases and doe-eyed obsession with Gavin has the cube on his phone damn near smoking and me opening the second to last box of egomaniac paraphernalia.

"Gavin, what's this stuff?" I ask as I pull a smaller box out of the inventory under the table.

"Oh, those are art prints. You should probably get them out and put them on display," he says as I slide the lid off of the box. There is a leather-bound book sitting on top of the stack of plastic sealed prints. It looks worn and well-loved, and it beacons me to open it.

"There's my sketchbook!" Gavin exclaims as he pauses mid-autograph. "I've been looking for that for weeks."

I put it back in the bigger box for now so I can get the art prints displayed with the rest of the dwindling merchandise, but I'm definitely going to be revisiting it. The sketchbook is clearly important to Gavin, so it must be a treasure trove of insight into his mind.

"Don't leave that out—someone will swipe it. Then I'd have to murder you and dump your body," he says over his shoulder. His threat only intensifies my urge to study each and every page.

For now, I look at each batch of prints as I start to organize them. The first image is of a Native American Chief wearing a full feather headdress and beaded chest plate. His face is old and grizzled, but there is so much life in his eyes—the detail is astounding, from the wispy blowing strands of hair to each perfectly notched bead.

The next set of art prints is a woman's face painted for Día de Los Muertos. Again, the detail is staggering. Her irises alone have three or four different levels of color. The other stacks of prints display the same artistry. There is a wolf, a cow skull, an angel, and a soldier.

I hardly get the prints arranged for sale before Gavin's client is handing me back the clipboard with his paperwork. I can tell he is antsy to get his tattoo underway and that Gavin's multitude of fans is unsettling to him.

"Alabama, can you get him prepped for me? The top of his arm needs to be shaved and cleaned. Disposable razors are in the top drawer." When he asks me this, it isn't really a question, nor does he look at me when he speaks. I'm a little surprised he wants my unskilled help, but there are still a handful of people that want to ask him questions or shake his hand, or bathe in his exhalations, or whatever.

By now, I've gotten somewhat used to the women fawning all over him. But more than anything, I'm ready for him to get started on the tattoo so the crowd can finally disperse. The longer he stands there, the more people will migrate over. Damn celebrities.

***

Once Gavin finally gets to work on the tattoo, it's not long until the convention goers begin to drift away. Let's face it, no one is here to see me, so people generally wait until he is available before swarming the booth. I have only scheduled a few appointments for him, and for the most part, I try to stay out of his hair—consequently, there is not much to do. I've already decided to plan my excursions away from the booth around the shows and demonstrations that I want to watch, so, for now, I'll stay put.

Remembering his sketchbook under the table with the boxes of inventory, I stealthily pick it up and then move the laptop so I can sit on my tiny allotted desk.

Gavin looks over when he realizes I'm sitting on top of the *chairless* reception table and then does a double-take when he notices my upper thigh. I cross my legs demurely, but after I see his reaction, I realize he can see the garter against the back of my thigh. Maybe he isn't as unaffected as he let on. That flash was an accident, but I'll make sure it happens again—very much on purpose.

He seems to make a point of not looking over at me, but that fact holds its own measure of power. That's right, Gavin. You focus on your work and try not to think about the bare skin that's exposed right above the lace of my thigh-high stocking. Yes, and don't forget that you were the one who fastened it for me.

As I page through his sketchbook, I see everything from dark and twisted demons to cartoonish figurines. He has drawn every conceivable type of animal, bird, and fish, but the drawings that really blow me away are the *people*. Rock legends, pop stars, athletes, presidents, religious leaders, movie characters, children, sexy women—everyone completely recognizable and drawn with such precision that I—

Wait.

What the…

Holy shit!

I feel like a solar flare just flashed over the convention center. It's scalding hot in here all of a sudden, and I can feel the flush of my skin like an over-heated electric blanket. All this suffocating heat happens the moment I turn the page and stare into my own face. The one that's peering out at me from the pages of Gavin's sketchbook.

I buzz through a few more pages of myself, some of them shockingly posed and nearly all of them missing some essential clothing, before I become profoundly self-conscious. I sincerely doubt he intended for me to see these.

It takes an extreme effort on my part to quietly close the book instead of studying every last detail of his drawings of me. I don't even know how many there are because I am so afraid to be caught looking at it.

I quickly busy myself with the merchandise, placing my body between the leather-bound book and Gavin's attention. I fiddle around re-folding t-shirts until I'm absolutely sure I can replace the sketchbook without being noticed. It feels heavy in my hand, as the constricted breath in my chest tries to work its way up and out my nose.

Gavin has drawings of me. Pages of them. Sexy and beautiful drawings pulled from his imagination...*of me.*

Chapter 16

Ok, the truth is that the Fuel Girls show was really cool. I'm going to give them that—but that's it. Because unfortunately, a couple of them have taken a shine to Gavin. Now, going out tonight will be a little more *high octane,* if you know what I mean.

The whole thing makes me want to gear up for a catfight because they hang on him like barnacles. Besides that, they are stunningly beautiful—and their show was crazy sexy, so my insecurities are at a level fifteen on a ten scale.

Not that Gavin is mine to claim, I know this, but I'm just saying I'd like to scrape off the extra hitchhikers. I was looking forward to the same group as last night, but that's not going to happen because Gavin has too many friends at the tattoo convention—and too many Fuel Girls.

Seeing my images in his sketchbook is messing with my head. Bad. I'm trying not to go to the place in my brain that wants to believe there's a chance for us because that only sets me up for disappointment. Colossal, heart splitting, disappointment.

Especially with beautiful pierced and tattooed women, who are clearly more his type than the stuffy, red-headed, advertising executive standing in my corner of the ring. I dressed as sexy as I dared to this morning—and had some definite success turning his head—but now we've all seen the Fuel Girl's pasty-covered tits and barely-there outfits, so any flashes of my garter have been vaporized from Gavin's memory.

The doors don't open until noon tomorrow, and we are only two blocks from the hotel, so I make a necessary decision and order a double vodka and soda. Actually, that's a lie. I order *two* double vodka and sodas because I will need to double fist it tonight simply to tolerate the additions to our group.

Unlike the place last night, there is no band playing, no good-natured dancing—no real distractions from the Gavin worship that I can't seem to get away from. Just a jukebox at the front of the bar and a rather thin crowd.

I have a hard time keeping the look of disgust off my face while I watch one of the Fuel Girls rub her crotch on Gavin's leg. The way he is sitting on the stool with one foot on the floor and the other on the bottom rung places his sloping thigh in the perfect position for her slowly grinding hips.

"Is this chick in heat or something?" I ask Phillip and Sunrise, but it's not really a question, it's more of a horrified declaration.

"I don't think he likes it. Look how he is trying to lower his leg," Sunrise points out. I'm unconvinced, these two women are throwing their sexuality at Gavin like spinning Frisbees, and he is probably fantasizing about the impending threesome to come.

The thought of him having sex with them tonight turns the liquor in my stomach sour. Would he bring them back to our room? Would he go M-I-A until tomorrow at the convention?

"Well, he better be careful, or she's going to leave some diesel on his jeans," I sneer. I'm aware that I sound really petty, and the vibe I'm giving off is more than a little jealous, but I can't seem to reel it in.

Phillip laughs at my comment harder than he should, then takes off to use the restroom while I strain my neck looking for our server. Another drink is clearly in order, along with something greasy and fried. Maybe some cheese sticks will distract me from the leg humping going on right next to me.

"Sunrise, how is the convention going for you? Are you staying pretty busy?" one of the Fuel Girls asks. It's better now that it's down to just two of them, but I still don't know their names.

"Yeah, I'm staying busy," she answers. I think Sunrise feels conflicted about talking to her knowing how I feel, but they clearly know each other, so I'm not going to say another nasty word about them.

"And you? What do *you* do for work?" the blonde Fuel Girl—not to be confused with the dirty-blonde Fuel Girl asks, as if she is interested in a single thing about me.

"Mostly, I just complain and make bad decisions," I answer her flatly. Strangely enough, I can feel Gavin's chuckle right next to me more than I can hear it. I know she is challenging me to establish female supremacy, but I don't want to talk about myself with her.

"Really? So, you're a pretty valuable employee then?" she asks while looking penetratingly into my eyes. Looks like she took my comment as aggressive rather than deflective.

"My value lies more in my inappropriate remarks than my work ethic," I say. Then, as if God Himself was trying to shut me up with a lightning bolt straight to my face, someone plays *Sweet Home Alabama* on the jukebox.

The riddle is solved when Phillip returns with a huge grin on his face and announces, "Man, I love this song!" then he grabs Sunrise and does a little dance spin-hug with her while she giggles.

"Not me. I think it's a dated, hick song that never should have been written, much less played," Dirty blonde says. I'm not sure if they know my name or not, so I'm withholding judgment on her snarky comment.

"Yeah? It's one of my favorites," Gavin says, and one of three things is happening. One, he is teasing me—which is most likely. Two, he is defending me. Or three, he is speaking in code to either Phillip or *me*. I have no idea which.

"Since you are at a tattoo convention and obviously into ink, why don't you show us some of your tattoos, *Alabama*?" Dirty-blonde says to me. Yep, they know my name, so that slam on the song was definitely strategic. I don't know if they are just trying to get rid of me, or if they thrive on dismantling other women. It's not important, I guess—either way, they are making me look stupid and ineffectual.

"It wouldn't be appropriate to show us her tattoos right now, but trust me—they are pretty special," Gavin says, and I'd say he was coming to my rescue except that he is still so chummy with them. He probably doesn't want to blow his shot at a three-way tonight.

"That's a real shame," blonde says as condescendingly as possible, but not to Gavin—she is speaking directly to me.

I'm feeling kind of vulnerable to these Fuel Girls, and I'm all done watching them eye-fuck Gavin and practically come on his leg, so I turn away from the three of them and say to Phillip and Sunrise, "I'm pretty tired. I think I'll just head on out. I will see you guys tomorr—"

"Hold it, Sassafras," Phillip states as he puffs up his chest and moves to stand in front of me. I don't say anything. I don't even look up into his eyes because I'm afraid my chin might quiver. Gavin is going to have sex with these women, and I can hardly stomach the thought.

Phillip seems to think better of his objection as he glances at the threesome and then lets out a sigh. He concedes, "Let me at least walk you back to the hotel."

Sunrise pulls me into a hug and says, "I'm gonna go pick out some songs, so we don't have to listen to *Jack and Diane* again. I'll see you tomorrow."

I don't say goodbye to Gavin because now the blonde has moved between him and me, completing her perfect trifecta and erasing me from his view and his mind.

When we step out onto the artificially lit Los Angeles sidewalk, I immediately feel the need to derail Phillip from his imminent line of questioning about Gavin and me.

"So, you and Sunrise seem to be hitting it off."

"Yeah. I love that girl. It's always good to catch up with her at these things," he says wistfully as he shoves his hands into his pockets. I knew they were something to each other, but I think he means it when he says he loves her.

"You only see each other at conventions?" I ask, surprised. "Why? You guys seem so much deeper than a hook-up here and there." This, of course, is none of my business, but if he is talking about Sunrise, then he is not asking about Gavin or filling my head with all sorts of unrealistic thoughts.

"We are thousands of miles apart, and both have successful businesses at home," he shrugs. "I adore her, but we could never be together, not really."

"I think that's the saddest thing I've ever heard," I say, slowing down a little more and turning to him.

"Sad, pathetic? Or sad, depressing?" he asks. The look on his face tells me he agrees with both assessments. As hard as Phillip's exterior looks, he has a gentleness to him that I find admirable.

"Actually, tragic is a better word. You guys are in perfect harmony together, yet you are going to let distance and logistics get in the way of being together."

"I don't disagree with you. It is pretty tragic, isn't it?"

"Yes, it is. And just think, if you always wait to run into her at tattoo conventions, what are you going to do if someone else scoops her up? What if the next time you attend a convention together—she's engaged to some other guy?"

He stops dead in his tracks, as though that scenario had never occurred to him. "You know, Alabama—I'm gonna suck on that for a bit, and I'll keep you posted." Typical of a guy not wanting to discuss his love life, he ignores the issue and starts walking again. Then he turns the tables on me.

"Speaking of being in harmony, what's up with you and Gavin?" he asks, and I scoff so loud, I almost choke on it.

"Are you insane? Did you happen to witness *any* of what was going on back there?"

"He may fuck one or both of them, but it doesn't take much to bang someone. He's not interested in them beyond getting his dick wet. He *is* interested in you, however."

"Does your brain actually follow that logic? In what world does fucking two other women indicate interest in me?" It's easier to bat down his words than it is for me to give any credence to what he says. I'm already holding back my tears until I'm alone, so it's counterproductive to entertain the idea that Gavin and I are a possibility.

"Did you hear how those women talked to me? He thought it was funny—"

"No, he didn't."

"Oh, no? Why didn't he stand up for me then?"

"Same reason I didn't. It's not our way. We didn't jump in with guns blazing because we knew full well that you could defend yourself."

"That's the biggest load of crap I've ever heard."

"No, it's not. Gavin needs someone with a backbone, or he'll walk all over them. The fact is, Alabama, he didn't want to swoop in and fight your battles for you. He wanted to know that you could fight your own."

"Ok then, while he's off screwing two strangers tonight, I'll give some thought to his genuine interest in me—how's that?" I'm lashing out, and it's far and away at the wrong person.

We both slow our pace again because we are nearing the front doors of my hotel. I'm already done with this conversation, though, and the more I think about Gavin having sex with the Fuel Girls, the more I want to cry.

"Sounds like we will both be thinking about our heart's desires tonight," he says with a laugh.

"Thank you for walking me safely to my hotel. You are a sweet man, you know that?" As I speak, I lean in to give him a hug because I need to cut this short. I can already feel the scratch of tears at the backs of my eyes.

"Have a good night, Alabama. We'll see you in the morning."

I don't know if he is referring to the fact that I won't be seeing Gavin tonight, so *they* will see me in the morning, or if he is speaking generally. Doesn't matter. Either way, I'm not looking forward to the next time I see Gavin. He'll be all rumpled and sexy—with two new notches for his headboard.

Now that I'm back inside the hotel lobby, I head to the bar to see if Sam is working. I need some company. Not sexual company, just conversational, to keep my mind off what's about to go down with Gavin and the Fuel Girls.

There are two bartenders working, neither of which are Sam, and a crowd that has long since dwindled. Now, only the diehards and the lonely remain. It's just as well, I suppose, alcohol has never solved any of my problems before.

I meant to grab one of Gavin's swag t-shirts to sleep in, but that isn't a problem anymore. I assume he will come back to shower all the sex off of himself before heading to the convention center tomorrow, so I'll make sure I'm up early enough that my attire isn't a problem.

Once I'm back in the room, I get as far as taking off my shoes, peeling off the leather halter, and replacing it with Gavin's tank top before I crumple into bed—skirt, stockings, garter, and all. This time I don't hold back my tears, and when I'm assailed by Gavin's scent on the sheets, I cry even harder.

I know I deserve this. I judged him based on his tattoos and tongue piercing, then jumped to conclusions about his level of sophistication. I gave no thought whatsoever to the fact that he is so much more than what's drawn on the surface.

Now that I have some understanding about the guy, I see exactly why my friends chose him for me. It turns out my picker *is* broken. I have never dated a guy who volunteers in a kid's cancer ward because I always pick selfish assholes.

Miles' words whisper to me in the darkness, *I have never been so disappointed in you.* Only now, it's worse because now they are my own words, and I did it to myself. To add to that disappointment is the fact that Gavin will be balls deep in two other women tonight. That visual is enough to bring on another bout of self-loathing. All I can think abo—

Holy shit! I hear a key card brush against the doorknob and then hear the thing turn. That mother-fucker brought them back here to rub my nose in it. My mind is spinning with thoughts of how I can possibly deal with this. It's obvious I've been crying, so all I can do is pretend to be asleep and hope I don't have to face them.

I'm only partway covered up, but all I have time to do before the door opens is drag a lock of hair across my face to hide my makeup smeared eyes. My back is to the entryway, but so is my mostly uncovered lower half. I'm fairly confident the skirt is covering my butt, but I hate that they will see me like this. They'll see me still dressed and 'asleep,' which means they will probably know I've been crying.

He closes the door quietly, and the fact that silence follows him into the room makes me think he's alone. It also hasn't been very long since I left, so unless he had a turbo threesome in the bathroom at the bar, he didn't shag the Fuel Girls.

I can hear him unzip his pants, slowly—one tooth at a time, then tug his shirt over his head. He is very careful to be quiet, so with any luck, he believes that I am sleeping. When I feel him inch into the bed, I hold my breath—I have to because otherwise, the frantic pace of my breathing will announce my wakefulness. Shit. This would be so much easier if I was turned away from him.

He's close to me. Close enough that I can feel the sizzle of his gaze all down the front of my body. I'm praying to God it's dark enough that he can't see my cry-face and smeared makeup.

When he gently swipes the hair away from my face and tucks it behind my ear, I'm so startled that I almost flinch with the unexpectedness of it. His touch is such a whisper that it shouldn't even register, but it does. Actually, the part that resonates the most is the tenderness of the whole thing.

"*I'm sorry,*" he breathes—more air than voice, and hardly audible at all. His gentle affection is enough to pool at the backs of my eyes with an inevitable flood of tears. All I can do now is sleepily turn away from him because there is no other way to hide the dampness about to breach my lashes.

The shift in position, although probably not super stealthy, puts my back to him. It also puts me closer than before. I'm so confused. I swear he takes joy in tormenting me, but these glimpses of a softer, less calloused man are enough to bring me to my knees.

He apologized to me, so that means he saw my streaked eye makeup. I hate that I'm so vulnerable right now. I don't know how to navigate this. And I certainly don't know where to put my feelings for him. Is his apology from a place of guilt? A place of caring? Is it an acknowledgment of the game he is playing? No matter what, he knows he hurt my feelings, and he knows I was crying.

I don't know what to do now, it's too late to take off these insufferable thigh-highs, so it looks like I'm sleeping in stockings and a garter tonight. Maybe if I wait until he's asleep, I ca—

Oh, my God! He just draped his arm over me. We aren't touching otherwise, but we are sort of spooning right now. His hand isn't touching me—just his forearm, so it's not really a sexual type of touch, more like a possessive one. I know I was snuggled up against him this morning, but I squirmed there while asleep. He is awake, and kind of holding me. He is *choosing* to touch me.

I wonder if his guard is down because he thinks I'm sleeping, or if his walls are starting to weaken. All I know is that he left the bar without his hook-ups in tow, his arm is around me, and I am wide fuckin' awake.

I lie here for ages waiting for him to fall asleep so I can take off my stockings. When his breathing finally levels out, and I know he is sleeping, I ease out of bed, peel off the discomfort, go clean my raccoon eyes, and then ever-so-gently raise the covers enough to slide back into bed.

Gavin is on his back now, with one forearm over his eyes and the other arm tossed carelessly back over his pillow. The position showcases his biceps and his naked torso. He's disarmed and recklessly sexy.

How I could have looked at this man and thought he was anything less than perfect, will forever be a mystery to me. Perhaps, even my greatest regret.

As I settle in next to him, he brings his arm down in such a way that I have to lift my head to accommodate it. The motion is so natural, that it's possible he did it on purpose. I didn't resist lifting my head for him because at first, I worried he would wake up if he met with resistance. Now I'm lying on his bicep, dangerously close to the side of his body, and I can't decide if I should get comfortable—or bail out.

Seemingly in answer to that question, he snugs up his arm and draws me flush against his body. I freeze for half a second before I give in and drape an arm over his abdomen. My heart is thrashing so hard it's like the whole bed has a rhythm of its own.

I don't know how I'm going to sleep like this. He is easily the most dangerous thing I have ever rested my cheek against. It's dangerous for me to hope. If I let myself acknowledge his current tenderness, or the drawings of me in his sketchbook, or the words Phillip had fed me like my last dying meal, I will end up getting my heart broken. No, not broken—shattered.

Whether or not Gavin is aware of what he's doing right now is of no consequence because once we are back in the light of day, everything will resort to business as usual. Gavin will shun me and go back to basking in the adoration of women everywhere. I'll be right back on the outskirts—tripping over the tongues of fans and Fuel Girls alike.

I wonder what my friends would say right now? Arden would probably tell me to turn my back to him and play hard to get, Miles would tell me to ease between his legs and take his cock in my mouth, and Ivy? Ivy would tell me to stay just like I am and trust that I'm on the right path. I'm not sure I can trust this path, but I am going to take her pseudo-advice and remain exactly where I am. I'll let nighttime unfold however it's going to, and then I'll deal with the repercussions later.

Right now, I'm going to let his warm body overwhelm my senses and drag me under. In sleep, we can lay down our swords and be together in restful oblivion.

Chapter 17

When the alarm on Gavin's phone goes off, I'm lying on my stomach using my forearms as a pillow, and he is turned toward me with his arm draped across my lower back. His face is no more than a breeze away from mine. In fact, when I open my eyes, he is looking straight into them and making no move to silence the alarm or remove his arm from where it rests across my body.

He is startlingly close and surprisingly unapologetic about it. His eyes give nothing away, but they are piercing—in a top of the food chain kind of way. His irises are blue, but stormy in that they look kind of gray as well. Steely. And confident.

What seems to be hovering in the air is less of a showdown than the desire to—what? Kiss me, maybe? This is the first time we have been this close and touching while both of us are unquestionably awake. It rattles me because as much as I want him to kiss me, the last thing I want is for him to do it *now*.

The stream of intimacy passes when he breaks eye contact and rolls backward to reach for his phone. The spell is apparently broken because then he flips off the covers and stands. He stretches his arms up the same way he did yesterday morning, but this time he is wearing white boxer briefs and sporting a massive erection.

He is facing me—and possibly even showing off because he knows I am watching him. He's grinning and looking at me when he adjusts his dick, not that there is anywhere for it to go, but some kind of an adjustment is clearly necessary. When he does, the elastic waistband pulls down to reveal two silver balls at the *very base* of his abdomen—

or, more accurately, sitting right above the root of his very prominent penis.

"Whatcha lookin at, Alabama?"

I still haven't so much as lifted my face off my arm pillows, and with the exception of some wild bed-head hair, there is little to disguise what must surely be an awestruck look on my face.

"I'm looking at a man that needs to go take care of business—apparently."

"*Take care of business?* Why-Alabama, what *ever* do you mean?"

I roll over and then lean back on my elbows, "It's that—or just sling it over your shoulder and haul it downstairs for breakfast." I catch his eyes dart down to my chest before making eye contact again.

"How about you go take a shower and leave the cock-slinging to me, Alabama. Plus, I don't carry it *over my shoulder*," he scoffs as he places his hands on his hips in a haughty, self-righteous stance, "That's what my backpack is for." His face splits into a completely disarming grin, and I have to look away, so he doesn't see the effect his sense of humor has on me.

I get up and smooth my skirt, making sure it covers my butt before I walk to the bathroom. I call out over my shoulder, "You've got ten minutes. I hope you brought a squeegee for cleanup."

After I shut the bathroom door behind me, I lean my hands against the counter and take a few deep breaths while studying the sink drain. I've spent the last five minutes looking at and talking about Gavin's dick. Between that and his wit, I may never be interested in another man ever again.

I'm not sure which basket to put his playfulness in. He seems to be warming to me while still keeping me at an emotional distance, which is still completely dangerous for me and my attraction to him. Is he just being friendly at this point? Is it more? His cues are so damn muddy and inconsistent.

I look up to face myself in the mirror, and all I can think is, *NOOOOO!* Because the last time I saw myself in this tank top, the mirror was all steamed up from Gavin's shower. Now—*now,* I can see my reflection with perfect clarity, and it's appalling.

No wonder Gavin kept looking at my chest, you can see my areolas and showy nipples straight through this ridiculous fabric. I've been so concerned with the spotty coverage of my lower half, I haven't spared a thought to the fact that I have been showcasing my tits to Gavin for two days.

Frustrated with my own obliviousness, I crank on the shower and peel off my clothes. Gavin prancing around with his mighty, engorged penis feels more strategic now.

While rinsing out my hair, I realize it's time to take this game to the next level, and I'm not talking about giving him little glimpses of my garter either.

***

By the time Gavin finishes in the bathroom, I'm already dressed. Today I am wearing my below-the-knee pencil skirt...and his tank top. The tank borders on obscene with the added snugness of being tucked in. And the thousand butterflies in my stomach are rioting against my braless display. I'm also wearing his suspenders, though I've not yet pulled them up and over my shoulders.

I attempt a breezy attitude while I finish blow drying my hair in the full-length mirror by the closet. My makeup is done, and my high heels are already on. I'm ready to take a well-placed shot across the bow.

Even though he has seen my tits through his tank top before, this is different. This is purposeful. And more explicit. *And* I've attached his own suspenders to the waistband of my skirt.

He is currently shirtless and freshly shaven with damp hair and the masculine authority of some sort of supreme being. He may be ignoring me in an effort to remain aloof, so as of now, he has not noticed his suspenders hanging from my hips.

As I run the flat-iron through my hair, Gavin approaches from behind. He stands there with his arms crossed over his chest and his eyes meeting mine in the reflection of the mirror.

"Those my suspenders, Alabama?"

"Yeah, they're cute, right?"

"I would not describe them as *cute*," he says as he squints his eyes at me.

"Sure they are. Look," I say as I turn around to face him, giving him an eyeful of dusty rose through sheer cotton. I shift my body enough to maneuver the straps to my shoulders and then stand up tall. "See?"

The suspenders partially obscure my brazen display, but not completely—and not enough to count on consistently throughout the day. What he doesn't know, is that I have zero intention of going to the convention with my tits out like this, but the thought is unnerving him, and I love it.

"Nope, still not cute. In fact…" he says as he slips two fingers under each suspender just below my collarbones, pulls them forward, and then releases them. They snap back harshly against my nipples, causing my eyelids to flutter closed with the sensation of the erotic slap. "…They're more distracting than anything else."

"So, you're saying you don't like them?" I ask, after a slow recovery from the humming of my nipples.

He spins me around so we are both facing the mirror, and while pressed up against me, he murmurs in my ear, "*I'm saying...*they are distracting." He continues to breathe against my ear and stare into my eyes while slipping a strap of the suspenders down my arm. He's undressing me, but only enough to torment.

He has a steel arm around my waist, and his gaze hasn't left mine when I whisper, "*Well, that's too bad,*" and then slip out of his hold. I have to get some distance because I am powerless against him. Until I can tell if he is flirting or simply trying to reclaim the upper hand, I would do well to avoid his carefully set snares.

***

When we arrive at the convention center, I'm still wearing his tank top and suspenders, but I added the black lace bralette underneath. Gavin teased me all through breakfast, saying things like, *it's a good thing you layered-up because people would have been asking for **your** autograph.* And, *Sunrise could have pierced your nipples without you even stepping foot in her booth.*

His shift from lustful man into teasing frenemy is all but complete, and any flirtatiousness has been extinguished.

Speaking of Sunrise, I've been giving more thought to having a few surface piercings done. If I decide to go for it, it wouldn't be here at the convention, I would need to wait until we get home. I want them hidden from view and don't relish the rest of this trip with piercings rubbed raw by my clothes.

Thinking about piercings makes me remember Gavin's silver balls right above his shaft, and how good he looked this morning. The fact that I know he trims his pubic hair and is packing an impressive *appendage* is enough to leach the saliva from my mouth. However, I *do* want to know more about those two little balls.

"What made you want to get pierced down there?" I ask as I indicate below his belt. He stops removing instruments from his Autoclave and looks at me.

"Are you asking me about my *pubic piercing*, Alabama?" The way he asks is like he is trying to embarrass me or incite a blush—both of which happen.

"It just seems like an unusual spot to be pierced, that's all," now I'm feeling shy because of the way he's still looking at me.

"Can you *really* not think of why I might have a piercing there?"

"I mean…I'm sure you have your reasons—"

"Hot damn! Gavin Rhodes, in the flesh! I've waited a long time for this, man!" says the incoming comet that is Gavin's first client of the day.

Once the formalities are dispensed with, paperwork is finished, and ink work started, I begin to drift further and further away from the booth. After two days of this, I know people tend to wait until he is not gloved and elbow deep in a tattoo before they purchase merchandise or schedule anything. And, with the exception of a few interested suitors that hang around well past their welcome, no one is here to see me, so my presence is not required.

"Not so fast, Hot Stuff," Gavin calls out. "I'm going to have time in between clients today to do some flash."

"O-kaaay," I say, not really sure what that has to do with me.

"I want you to go through the people from this convention who signed up for my mailing list and find me two people that are interested in quick, easy tattoos."

I make my way closer to him so I can see his progress, ever mindful of threatening his sterile field. "I'm just supposed to pick someone?" I ask.

"No, you'll need to ask some qualifying questions first, and contacting them by email is not exactly efficient. It will take some time."

"What kind of qualifying questions?"

"Do they have an image with them? Is it a size that can be completed in a short timeframe? Have they been drinking? Stuff like that. I can only do so much with the time I have between clients. Plus, flash is basic work, and not everyone wants basic work."

"Got it. Weed out the partiers with thinned blood. And determine who among your minions wants sorority letters or a tribal armband. I'm on it." Gavin looks down, but not before I see the smile he's trying to hide.

I suppose this is as good a time as any to input the names from this convention into a spreadsheet. That way, it will at least be organized, and he can compile it with his master list. Too bad he has seven or eight different files dedicated to his mailing list—it's hard to say which one is the master list.

After comparing the files and finding no overlap and even less consistency, I determine that I'm dealing with fifty-eight signups from this convention and thousands upon thousands from God-knows-where-else.

"Do you *have* a file with your master list?"

"Nah, I just start a new one for each convention."

"You don't have them compiled? How do you work with so many different lists?"

"I don't," he says, and from an advertising perspective, his words burn my ears.

"I'm sorry, *what*?"

"I don't even know why I have them. I don't do anything with mailing lists."

"For fuck's sake, Gavin! You need me more than I thought." He answers me with a non-committal snort and then tucks his head back into his work.

I spend the next two and a half hours creating a master file, linking it to his website, and fielding potential flash clients. He is sitting on a goldmine as far as marketing goes, never mind the branding aspect that is almost completely untapped. His website doesn't even sell merchandise or offer promos.

I pick the first two flash clients that I deem appropriate—one guy and one girl. Then I have them fill out their paperwork, and prep each of them by cleaning and shaving the work area. I make copies of their flash art and then send them on their way after leaving me with their mobile numbers.

"Gavin, do you think your receptionist would want to make more money hourly by processing and packing up e-commerce orders?"

"Sure, she's bored a decent amount of the time. But I don't sell merchandise online." Because I do it behind his back, he misses the incredulous miming of having my mind blown.

Short of texting the flash clients when Gavin is ready to see them, I don't do anything for the rest of the day except design him a new website that I will present to him later. He doesn't have to use mine, but he would be an idiot not to. Design is not my forte, but marketing *is*, and I can help him.

I suspect his lack of a social media presence, e-commerce website, and useable mailing list have more to do with him being overwhelmed rather than a lack of desire. He has a mailing list, he just doesn't know what to do with it. And although he has merchandise made for him, I can almost guarantee he fumbles through the inventory and reorder process. The fact is, this could all be so much easier and streamlined for him.

It's not until he is working on his last client of the day that he takes actual notice of me taking pictures with my phone. They are mostly artistic shots of stuff like his tattoo machine or the little plastic cups of ink, but I can do some cool stuff with them like blurring the background or adding texture. The ones I take of him are on the sneak because he keeps crossing his eyes when he knows I've directed my phone at his face.

Anyway, I'm so focused on my mission, when Sunrise enters the booth with the same intensity of a high school drumline, she startles me.

"Gavin, come—your guy is a finalist for Best Tattoo of the Day!" Gavin's back is to us as he labels the sterilization sleeves for the Autoclave, but he remains fairly non-pulsed about the whole thing. He casually finishes what he is doing and then turns to face us.

"Well, alright then, let's go."

***

For the second time this convention, Gavin wins *Best Tattoo of the Day*. The tattoo that won this time was done in color. His black and gray work is amazing, but I've never seen anything like his color tattoos. I'm struck by how humble he is about the whole thing too. I get the impression that he likes being the best, but doesn't like to announce it or be showy about it.

Once he's off the stage, he only puts up a minimal fight when I start snapping selfies of the two of us. He even draws me in close and puts his tongue in my ear, which made for a really cute pic. In it, I'm caught in an open-mouth laugh while he faces me with his tongue in my ear, and his eyes turned to the camera looking mischievous.

One of Gavin's tattoo buddies tells us everyone is going out after everything gets broken down and packed up, and because I'm starving-hungry, I decide to be very helpful in the break down process.

The convention doors were supposed to close at eight tonight, but there are still some stragglers as we take down the banner and pack up everything getting shipped home. The convention was a success if you gauge it by the stupid amount of money Gavin made, but also because he doesn't hate me anymore. He is not necessarily a *fan*, but the burning animosity is gone.

After we completely finish packing up, I crack open the laptop. Gavin is giving everything a final wipe down with germicidal wipes when I call him over.

"What do you think about this?" I ask when I show him the website I designed. He does a double-take when he sees his logo and name along with a really cool picture of him from the side. I hold up a finger for him to wait, as I navigate to the product page.

"You can set it up to reorder when you get down to a certain amount of inventory, and it creates your mailing labels for you." He leans in, surprised I have his current merchandise itemized and described on the page already. "I also have a mailing list service merged with your site, links to your social media profiles, and an—"

"I don't have any social media profiles," he says as he leans in and navigates back to the home page. I took the bio from his old, janky site but it looks a thousand times better now.

"Sure you do, look," I show him all the new profiles I set up. "They aren't live, but I wanted you to see the potential."

"Damn, Alabama. Did you do all of this today?"

"Yes. And look at this, I want to show you an example of something you could send to your mailing list." Before I click on the navigation bar, I ask him, "What do you think is the most frustrating thing for your clients right now?"

"Easy. Waiting so long to get in."

"That's what I thought, so look at this." The page gives his clients a chance to win airfare, hotel, and a six-hour tattoo for $50. I worded it so 50% of that price would be a donation to one of two charities. I chose both charities strategically, one is Susan G. Komen, and the other is The Children's Hospital, both of which I know he is involved with just from his dating profile pictures.

"I don't know if you are aware, but your mailing list has more than 17,000 people on it. With this one promo, you would cover the costs associated with the tattoo, and make some hefty charitable donations."

"Damn."

"You don't have to inundate your mailing list with spam either, maybe send something twice a year. Throw them a bone, give them an opportunity to get in sooner."

"This is incredible."

"I know, now let's go eat—I'm starving."

Chapter 18

Having been chosen as the designated hangout spot for the final evening of the tattoo convention, the bar is crowded. Not just crowded, but spilling over, and feisty. The clientele of this place is best described with a Yin and Yang symbol. On one side of the symbol are the preppy frat boys, and on the other, are the leather-clad bikers. The women here run the spectrum, but I'm fine with any of them that don't smell like gasoline.

Gavin parts the crowd and arrives back at our bar table with five or six shots held recklessly in each hand. I can't tell what they are, but I'm fairly certain they will put hair on my chest.

Hands from every direction divest him of the shot glasses while spilling a healthy amount onto the dinged-up tabletop. On an empty stomach, the slug of burning hellfire will go straight to my head, so I need to order food, and soon.

I'm blinking away the tears caused by swallowing that nasty shot when Gavin makes a sweeping scan of the crowd and then announces his assessment.

"I'm kind of sick of the bar scene." He doesn't say it with any passion, or even disappointment. It's more like his shining declaration of boredom. A few of his friends scoff and then promptly ignore the unpopular sentiment, but Sunrise lights up.

"Me too. Let's get out of here and order a pizza," she suggests. I'm thrilled to leave the bar as long as it involves food. I don't get a chance to answer, though, because Phillip loudly agrees with her and then grabs her face for an impromptu kiss.

"Our hotel has a rooftop pool," Gavin says as he stands up, apparently deciding for all of us.

***

The evening air is crisp up here. It's too chilly to swim, which proves God answers prayers because I was praying like a zealot that I wouldn't have to get in the pool.

For its part, the hot tub has fallen down on expectations too because it's warm, but only just. None of us want to get in a merely warm hot tub, so we sit around the edge of it, dipping our lower legs and finishing off the delivered box of pizza.

I suppose I have the same rules we are breaking to thank for the fact that the four of us are alone up here. But also, for the hot tub timer that ensures compliance of said rules.

It's Sunday evening, so the pool closed an hour ago. Had we come last night, the rooftop terrace would have been open until midnight, and someone would be mixing drinks behind the bar. As it stands now, the pool is brightly lit, and the row of four cabanas sit empty except for the double lounge chair and short stack of towels in each one.

I'm not one for breaking the rules, but I'm also not one to stand up to three other people who have no such qualms, so here we are. A pencil skirt may not be the best option for sitting on the edge of a hot tub, but it's better than the alternative—which is swimming naked in the pool.

"So, Alabama, Gavin tells me you two met on a dating site, is that right?"

***

Gavin has this look every now and then where he tips his chin down but keeps his eyes locked on mine. In those moments, he looks like an apex predator braced and ready to pounce. But there is also a certain haughtiness to it, like he outranks everyone else. That look always seems as though he's establishing himself as the Alpha, or maybe reminding us that we are only visitors in his world.

The problem with that is that I haven't gotten to where I am at work by letting people designate me the omega. I have a trait that's inherent to my being, and that trait makes me want to push back. I want to challenge his authoritative position. Not that I don't respect it, I just don't buy into the superiority it imparts.

If I were to analyze my instinct to challenge him, purely from an armchair psychiatrist's perspective, of course, I would say I'm trying to claim the footing my parents denied me while growing up. But I'll let a therapist sort all that out at a later time.

Right now, we are sitting across from each other on opposite sides of the hot tub. So his chilly, deep blue gaze is mostly trained on me. The naturally superior, Alpha one. The conversation has stalled a bit too, but no one seems to want to fill the empty space.

Sunrise looks at Gavin—with that look on his face, and then back to me before suddenly wanting to get out and dry off her legs. His look apparently spoke to her—or maybe it was the same look mirrored on my face that made her decision, but she didn't waste any time pulling the lever on her ejector seat.

"I've had enough of this lukewarm water, what about you?" her question is directed at Phillip, and it lands like a bullwhip before he too jumps up. For a few minutes, Gavin and I just watch them right their clothes and gather up whatever personal belongings they brought with them. If you ask me, I think they are in just as big of a hurry to be alone as they are to leave us to our sexually charged showdown.

I like them both, quite a bit actually, but I'm not sad to see them disappear through the huge glass doors. There is a quiet left behind them that sounds like nothing more than a summer's breeze. The city noise is well below us, so the only real sound to carry on that breeze is the buzzing restraint keeping my body from pouncing on Gavin.

I should be pretty relaxed now that the hustle and bustle of the convention is over, but I'm not—not at all. I feel like an overfilled, pinched shut balloon that someone's about to let go of. And the fact that I want to vault over the water and find out what Gavin's tattoos taste like is not helping my state of mind.

Now that we are alone, I feel reckless. And the look on his face isn't helping matters. Nope—not one bit.

"Why are you looking at me like that, Alabama?"

"I'm not looking at you in any particular way. I just haven't figured you out yet, that's all." I break eye contact for a second because it feels too intimate with just the two of us up here. When our eyes meet again, the same intimacy hovers, but there is caution there too.

"No? What would you like to know?" He is almost purring, but it also feels like he is setting a trap for me to mindlessly walk into.

"Offhand? I don't know—lots of stuff, I guess."

"MmHmm," he mumbles, but it still sounds like a challenge as he drags his palm across the scruff on his chin. "Like my pubic piercing, *Alabama*?" His eyes are sharp again, and the color of the churning ocean.

I try to remain undaunted by the thought of those two silver balls right above his shaft, but the way he says my name tickles the inside of my pelvis. We are both stone-cold sober, and he is directing the conversation down a sexy path. This might be unrecoverable for me because I won't be able to go back to how it was before introducing this level of intimacy.

"Tell me about it," I say. It sounds shy, but I'm about ready to ask him to show me—and that's as far away from shy as I get.

"What do you want to know about it? *Hmm?* Do you want to know how the balls would feel rubbing against your clit? Maybe you're wondering if the metal would feel cool pressed against your bare, sensitive skin? Or if the balls would be warm and wet?" I give a needy sigh in response to his words that makes me want to hold my head under the water and drown myself.

"You've never been with someone who has piercings have you?" he asks, though he knows good and well what my answer is. He's got that look on his face again, and his gaze is burning through his dark lashes. I don't answer him, so he keeps talking.

"So, you've never felt the metal ball of a tongue piercing glide up the crease of your pussy?" he asks, unflinching and as intent as ever. I hold his gaze but don't say anything. There is not a whole lot *to* say.

"Never felt the warm barbell caress your silky lips apart, spreading you open for someone's wet and eager tongue?" He leans forward, but only to further emphasize his taunting. I still don't look away, but his words have a serious effect on my shaky composure.

"You've never felt the steady flutter of slick metal against your sensitive clit?" He pauses and looks deeper into my soul, his eyes beseeching, "Or felt the erotic pressure of it when someone licks and then gently sucks your little pearl into their mouth?" his voice is low, but the rasp of it carries across the surface of the water. All of his words are carefully spaced out and enunciated with a tormenting rumble. Jesus, he's a predator toying with his prey.

"No," I whisper, still not taking my eyes off of him. He's under my skin. He knows it, and I know it—and he didn't even get close enough to touch me.

"Yeah? Well, that's a shame," his voice is clear and strong now, as he wipes his hands on his denim covered thighs and starts to get up. "We better head in before we get locked out here for the night." His demeanor has done a complete one-eighty.

Holy shit.

He was fucking with me.

***

Back in the room, he polishes off a bottle of water before grabbing the back of his collar and tugging the shirt over his head. In the elevator, he had rambled on about everything he wanted to do before our flight out tomorrow night and gave no indication of any interest in me whatsoever. Not a single acknowledgment of the state of my panties.

He might still be punishing me, but he is going to suffer too. I know he's interested, he's just playing with his food first. That hot tub stunt was on another level, but as always, I will rise to the occasion.

I know his ego is having a hard time with the fact that I told him he wasn't my type and basically insinuated he wasn't good enough for me. I'm not sure if he wants to hear me voice my changed feelings and admit how wrong I was, or if he will eventually let it go—after I've suffered an adequate amount—of course.

Chapter 19

When I come out of the bathroom, Gavin is wearing navy athletic pants and nothing else. He is also lying on top of the covers watching CNN. His eyes follow me, but the rest of his body holds its position—now, rigid as a statue and leaning back against a stack of pillows.

There is something smoky in his gaze too. Something lust-filled, and insatiable. He is interested—of this, I am certain. I'd counted on his buy-in when I put on this outfit. My skimpy panties are really just a tiny scrap of satin and a bunch of fragile looking crisscrossing straps. I'm also wearing the deep purple, see-through, mesh top. I say *top* because the damn thing is so short, but I think it had aspirations of being a teddy at one time.

I walk over to the ice bucket and scoop some into a glass. The one hundred percent calculated act puts me with my back to Gavin, and standing right next to the TV. He couldn't avoid seeing my skimpy panties if he tried to.

Then, of course, I bend over to get a bottle of water from the mini-fridge before turning around and propping my ass against the wooden console. I watch him stare at me for a long minute before I pour the water into the glass.

I'm not completely comfortable with my body, but for the moment, he's looking at my breasts. They seem to be doing their job of distracting him from any of my naked insecurities, so I pause here and sip my water.

"Pretty amazing, right?" I ask, before setting my drink down. He doesn't respond, but his eyes slowly drag up my body until they meet my gaze.

"The tattoo convention. It was pretty amazing, right?" I ask with the twitch of a smile to my lips. No matter how the convention played out, the fact that he's gone from calling me a *cunt*, to wanting to split me open with his penis is amazing in itself. As far as I'm concerned, the rest of the convention is pretty insignificant.

"It was ok," he says as he maneuvers himself under the blankets. "Can you hit the lights when you're done? I'm beat." Then, that fucker rolls to his side like he's going to sleep. What? How much longer is this stupid game going to go on? Never mind.

I will break him.

"You got it. *Sweet dreams, Gavin,*" I say pleasantly as I stand here and fume. He wants to prove his moral supremacy by breaking me. He is waiting for me to cave in or surrender. I will too. If this ridiculousness goes on much longer, I will raise the white flag. He'd never let me forget it, but still, all this nonsense would be over.

I still have one more trick up my sleeve, though, and I'm going to have some fun with my last-ditch effort. The fact is, I'm not going to let him ignore me right now.

I slide into bed and scoot as close to his back as I can. I also shimmy my arm under his, so I have it draped over his side. He tenses up, but only for a second. Kind of like he's trying to work out my angle, but senses an ambush just the same.

It's dark in the room, so my sense of touch and smell are acutely aware of his closeness. If I turned my head a tiny fraction, I could easily kiss his back—right between his shoulders. Where his skin is untouched by ink but seductively close to it. The ache to brush my lips against his skin is strong, but I can't.

Kissing is too intimate, and I don't want to use intimacy as a weapon, not now—not ever. When we finally kiss, it will be when all the games are behind us, and we both submit to the other. When the hurt feelings and harsh words have morphed into something sweet. Right now, we both have a leery respect for the other, but the walls he's built have been fortified over weeks of time, and heaps of hurt and anger.

He and I have made some definite strides over the last few days, and although we didn't come together under normal circumstances, I still think we are building toward something that could be pretty special.

Obviously, his interpretation of not being my type is that he's undesirable to me. Although he is taking this way too far, and having too much fun proving that he *is* desirable, I can understand why he's doing it.

Instead of playing into his game, what I should have done is let my guard down and let him see my attraction to him. Instead of hiding my growing feelings behind a mask of indifference, I should have been vulnerable. I should have gushed over how amazing his work is. I should have laughed at his wit instead of rolling my eyes. I should have let him know how scandalously sexy he is instead of just melting on the inside.

If I had allowed myself to be vulnerable, we wouldn't be playing this cat and mouse game. He would be facing me, and we would be sharing our first kiss right now.

He's not sleeping, but he's also not making any attempt to turn around or talk to me. As I anticipate my next move, the blood starts to churn through my body, and my breaths speed up. I'm nervous about pushing things to the next level—but I'm going to nonetheless. I can't hesitate much longer, but the anxious rattling in my stomach will not relent.

My forearm is already poised over his waist, but I'm about to touch his abdomen with my hand. It will definitely be a sexual advance, and depending on his reaction, I may even push a little more. I only need him to crack—maybe not completely, but at least open himself up to me a little bit. I need him to drop the façade.

Sex is not the endgame. Not tonight anyway, because I want to be more than a cum receptacle for him. If we have sex tonight, it will be because I seduced his dick. But I want his mind and his heart too. I need both of those before I give him my body.

My pulse is strumming aggressively through my veins, but it's like blood is only pumping to my vital organs, leaving my extremities hollow and unnourished. I have to make up my mind soon. It's time.

When I begin to feather my fingertips over his abs, I hear his breath catch in his throat, like he is perching on the edge of something. I don't want him to stop me—I need to open this door, but his hesitation loiters in the corners of my mind, and doubt starts to seep in. It warns me to be careful—to guard my heart above all else.

He doesn't turn or speak, so, with a little trepidation, I drift my fingers lower. His skin is soft against the firm muscles as my hand explores and learns the terrain of his body. It might be my imagination, but now more than before, I can smell the warmth on his skin. It's working in tandem with my bold advance to fuse us together.

I delve even lower, sliding my fingers under his waistband and finding the forbidden, neatly trimmed area. I want to pause for a second to collect myself, but I'm afraid my own hesitation would come off as timid, so I continue down to the silver balls.

I toy with them for a bit before I hear his long exhale. It's like he'd been holding his breath and only now is breathing again. Beneath his skin, I can feel the bar that links the balls, and I know I'm caressing him right above his shaft. The awareness of that fact is strong enough to be its own personality in the room with us.

Touching his piercing like this makes me imagine how the balls *would* feel against my clit. The image of him grinding his pelvis against my body while we have sex is almost enough for me to acknowledge the hard penis resting against the back of my hand. In this instance, there is nothing but the pure strength of will separating the two of us.

Gavin still hasn't said anything, and besides the creeping up of his erection, he hasn't moved a muscle. I speak before taking time to analyze the repercussions of what I'm about to say.

"I want to taste it, Gavin," I whisper, and even I am not sure if I'm referring to his piercing or his prominent dick. I feel like I'm panting, yet taking in no air. In fact, I'm not sure there is any air left in the room.

He still doesn't respond, so I draw his hip towards me, easing him to lie down on his back. Now he rolls over, but not completely of his own volition, so I still feel like he might be trying to avoid this. I maneuver my body over his thigh as he lies back fully with his wrists crossed and covering his face.

It's a compromising position for us, but I have no intention of giving him head tonight. He needs to let me know he wants me first, and not just for sex or a blowjob. His erection is straining against his athletic pants, so I shift it aside with my chin and lower his waistband enough to dust his piercing with the lightest of kisses. I feel him groan—it's not at all audible, but I feel it as though he shouted it across the room.

I get braver after the groan and start to flick my tongue over the two balls. The intense awareness I have about his steel-hard penis resting against my neck and jaw makes it feel hot up against my skin—even though it remains beneath the fabric. It's rigid and insistent and I'm completely struck by the *heat* of it.

I tickle and scratch my fingernails down the tautness of his torso, stopping my hands on his hips where I hold him in place. His body has started to writhe but only on the inside, and I can taste the torment as it radiates off of him.

I pay special attention to his piercing as I flick my tongue against it and then lightly tug one of the balls with my teeth. I'm also kissing and nibbling the area above it, moving towards his belly button and peppering his pronounced V-line with doting attention as well.

At this point, he has relinquished all control. He's not fighting what I'm doing—but he's also not participating, and this is as far as I'm willing to go without his buy-in.

With a final brush of my lips against his lower abdomen, I maneuver myself up his body to whisper in his ear, "Now I know all about your pelvic piercing. Sleep well, Gavin."

There is a moment when it seems like time stands still. Gavin hasn't moved, and his arms remain over his face. I wish I knew what he was thinking because that would make everything so much easier. When he remains quiet, I roll to my side and squeeze my eyes shut. It feels like everything is on pause while I lie here in limbo. Purgatory, really.

After what feels like an eternity, he lightly drags one finger down my arm—shoulder to wrist. Then he rolls me to my back as my body explodes with goosebumps from his searing touch. He is braced on his elbow as he swipes the hair away from my cheek with his thumb. His shadowed face is only inches from mine when he speaks in a low voice.

"What about all the things I want to know? Huh, Alabama?" My skin feels like it can no longer contain the riot bubbling just beneath the surface, and I can scarcely find words to respond to him.

"What is it you want to know?" my voice is a whisper of air, not words at all, and I find that it's me who is trembling on the inside this time. It seems he has found his stance, and it's a commanding one.

"There are all sorts of things I want to know," he pauses while his fingers find the lace hem at the bottom of my plum teddy. He eases his hand underneath and speaks with a quiet rumble.

"For example, I want to know how sensitive your nipples are—I need to know if I should be gentle with them…or rough." His palm, ever so gently, grazes across the tips of both bare nipples. His touch is so light, it's *almost* imperceptible.

"I want to know if you'll be shy when I spread your thighs apart and stare at your naked, unobstructed body while it's so blatantly revealed to me. I want to know if you'll squeeze your eyes shut when I bury my face in the warmth between your legs." His voice is soft, and his continued caress is maddening with its near *absence* of touch.

Right now, I'm only breathing through a series of gasps as his palm skims my body, leaving nothing but need and the residual tickle from his feather touch in its wake.

"I want to know how you taste when I spread you apart with my tongue. I want to know if your thighs will tremble from the intensity of your orgasms. I want to know how you sound when you come. Do you stifle a throaty groan?"

I'm barely breathing as he brushes his palm lightly over my stomach and breasts. Again, his touch is nothing more than the tiniest of whispers—hardly making contact at all.

"…Or do you wrench your head back and cry out?"

"*Gavin,*" I whisper as I arch my back, encouraging more contact with his hand, but gaining none.

"Shhhh. I want to know what your tiny gasp sounds like against my ear when I enter you for the first time." He continues to caress my bare skin, light as a feather, but completely owning my body just the same.

"I want to know what it feels like to have you spasm around my cock. And, Alabama? I want to know if you'll scream my name or call out to God."

"*Gavin,*" again in a pained whisper, but nothing follows. I'm not even sure what I want to say at this point. My body is lit up like *never* before, and I can't concentrate to save my life.

"Open your legs, *Alabama,*" his voice is commanding, and it overwhelms all my systems at the same time. Each nerve fiber in my body misfires and short circuits all at once.

Open your legs, Alabama.

He slides his hand down my body, further encouraging me to spread my thighs. The skimpy panties are hardly a barrier as his fingers slip underneath them and between my legs. His touch is like a warm, melty jolt of static electricity.

His composure slips a little when he drops his chin to his chest and groans, "*Jesus,* you're so wet." And then his fingers start to move against me.

His ministrations are confident, yet darkly poetic as the buildup over the last few days comes raining down on me all at once. The moan starts way in the back of my throat, with little awareness of anything except the kaleidoscope of sensations he is providing.

At first, he focused almost solely on rubbing my clit, but when I started to squirm against the oblivion he offered, he slowed his movements and began to learn the other intricacies of my body.

I know he's watching my face, and under his scrutiny, all I can do is close my eyes and bite down on my lip. I can't look at him right now. It's too intense. He's so attentive, he'd see directly into my soul.

I'm climbing higher and faster, and when I let go of my lip to release a restrained exultation, his mouth is on mine. An instant is all it takes for me to become his. Just his kiss. It's that simple.

For a moment, his kiss is tender—maybe even slightly restrained. But almost as soon as his lips meet mine, my orgasm takes hold, and I grind a whiny, shuddering moan directly against his kiss. He takes it all and then gives it back to me, laced in something sweet—something that feels a little like adoration.

To claim my mouth at the moment of climax like that was intensely powerful. It elevated our first kiss to a place that's hard for me to express. It was almost like he was giving me something special, but he was also taking something special in return.

I've never been moved to tears by an orgasm before, but my eyes moisten, and my breath catches in my throat. To be fair, I don't think my emotional state is due entirely to my release. I think it's because I needed him to crack, and he did. We did. With his kiss, we cracked together, and it's beautiful.

Had he not kissed me, I would think this was purely physical. But his kiss—this kiss is so much more. It's unhurried and passionate. It's full of raw emotion and words left unspoken.

When he brings his hand up to cup my jaw, the tenderness of the act is only dulled by the raunchy fact that I can feel my own wetness on his fingers. The gesture is dirty and erotic and perfect.

He pulls back a fraction as he drags his moistened fingers across my bottom lip. Then his mouth is back on mine before he even removes his fingers. In this way, we share my taste, which only seems to magnify his desire for more.

When he moves his hand behind me to cradle my head, I can't help but feel like the gesture is protective—possessive even. For him to behave in this way toward me is everything I could have hoped for and more.

As the night wears on, our mouths harmonize perfectly together, but neither of us takes the next step. No groping hands, no clumsy removal of clothes, no advances toward sex at all. We just fit together perfectly, and we kiss.

When he backs his head up to look into my face, his eyes are drunk, and his smile is genuine. His emotional distance has evaporated, and an aspect of sincerity has taken over.

"Well, I suppose that answers one of my questions anyway," he says through a rumbly laugh. My own eyes are dizzy and swimming with lust, and my dopey smile mirrors his. Instead of discussing the fact that I moan instead of scream, I raise my head off the pillow to join our lips again. I'm not done kissing him yet. I don't think I'll ever be done kissing him.

By the time dawn begins to shine through the crack in the curtains, my face is raw from his stubble. Hours of making out like teenagers still has not progressed to more, and the significance of that is not lost on me. It means a lot that he, too, did not want last night to be about the raw carnality of sex.

I'm not too sure either of us could have stopped the forward momentum had advances been made, but somehow, we both sensed the unspoken boundary. Fucking someone is easy. Caring about them is something else entirely, and combining the two requires finesse beyond the unchecked greed of desire.

When he tucks me against his side and whispers, "We need to sleep," against my temple, my eyes have already grown powdery with exhaustion. I nod in agreement, but my hold on him doesn't loosen as I nestle against his warm, welcoming body. My smile is still in place as we nod off to sleep, and I have never been so grateful for second chances.

Chapter 20

I wake up as Gavin tries to slip his arm out from under me. It feels like late morning, but with the curtains closed, it's hard to tell. I'm still groggy, but memories of last night suffuse my body and settle in the happy curl of my lips.

"I'm sorry, I was trying not to wake you," Gavin says as he kisses my forehead and then slides his body out from under my arm. "Go back to sleep, it's only been a few hours." I nod and close my eyes, grateful to get more rest after a long and wonderful night.

When I hear him start the shower, I dump the exhaustion from my eyes and sit up to look at the clock. It's not even eight-thirty yet. We *have* only been asleep for a few hours. I lie back down and decide to deal with whatever this is when I wake up.

Gavin eases back into bed with me, freshly showered and with droplets of water still clinging to him if the way my clothes fuse to his body is any indication. He spoons me from behind, hugging me pleasantly against his body and brushing his lips against my ear as he whispers to me.

"That's much better."

It takes me a few seconds to realize what he means, then I turn around and burrow into his chest, chuckling softly while I inhale the masculinity of his damp skin.

"You are such a gentleman," I manage to get out before burying another round of giggles into his armpit.

"You have no idea," he deadpans. "But now I can sleep next to you without the pressure of the Mariana Trench in my nut sack," he chuckles into the darkened room as he snugs up his grip on me.

The last couple of hours must have been rough on him because he's asleep before I'm even done thinking about him masturbating in the shower. I wonder if he uses quick, shallow strokes, focusing on the head, or long, deep pulls that tug on his whole shaft? I also wonder what he thinks about when he jerks off? And, when he comes, do the tendons in his neck strain, or does that one forehead vein bulge?

The next time I wake up, I feel rested. Right away I notice that Gavin is awake too because he twirls a lock of my hair around his finger. He must feel my eyelashes brush against his chest because he abandons the lock of hair and grabs a handful of it instead. Then he carefully tugs my head back so he can drop a kiss on my lips.

I am not a morning kisser—never have been, but something about him not caring about our breath makes me smile. We slept threaded together, which is unusual for me. Typically, I like my own space when I sleep, but with Gavin, I feel like I could be inside of him, and it still wouldn't be close enough.

"Morning," he says in a husky morning voice that makes my insides feel warm and unguarded.

"Good morning," I say as I unwind myself from him and sit up. I have intentions of getting up to brush my teeth, but he has different ideas as he hauls me on top of him, cowgirl style—but with a blanket between us, so it's less wicked.

"Fuuuck, just let me look at you for a minute," he says with his hands on my waist, making the flimsy fabric cling a little tighter to my body. Last night I felt like a seductress in this outfit, but this morning I feel overexposed and a bit self-conscious.

Trying to divert his attention, I ask, "What do you want to do today?" His eyes drag upward until he looks me in the eyes. When you add his hungry gaze to his rumpled hair and bare chest, it's impossible not to think about sex. The three of those things combined form a triad of lust, and my spread-legged position only amplifies that feeling.

"We have a late flight, so we have all day—" his hands slide around to grip my mostly bare ass, "I think we should go back up to the pool."

"I don't have a swimsuit," I say. I'll be honest, I'm a little disappointed his train of thought went to the pool because mine went straight to having sex all day, especially after his hands grabbed my butt.

"Me neither, but we *are* in a budding metropolis. We'll go buy some," he laughs before continuing, "We can pick up some food and drinks, grab one of the cabanas..."

I smile and nod in response. I love that there is no hint of the snarky, standoffish guy who kept dousing me with varying levels of dislike. It's like the dam broke. We kissed all night, and now there are no walls left to defend.

"Well, let's go then," I say as I drag him forward into a sitting position. "We're burning daylight."

Chapter 21

It took Gavin three and a half minutes to pick out a pair of swim trunks, but I am more discerning in the matter and take no less than eight options into the fitting room with me. It's a small surf shop, and Gavin soon tires of perusing the merchandise and trying on sunglasses, so he takes up a conversation with the owner right outside the dressing room.

"Come on now, let's see it," he encourages. Honestly, this suit is not even in the running, and I wouldn't have a problem showing Gavin, but the shop owner is out there too.

I try to adjust the top as much as I can to maximize the coverage it's attempting to provide, but the suit is built for a fifteen-year-old, so the effort is futile. I slide the curtain open, but I don't dare step out, and I most certainly don't dare to turn around.

Both guys are facing me. The owner has his battered flip flops planted in a wide stance, and his artificially white teeth over accentuate his approving smile. Gavin looks scandalized and like he wants to throw a giant tarp over me.

The owner whistles and gestures for me to turn around, while Gavin swallows hard and shakes his head in a slow rejection that reads like a booming, *absolutely-fucking-not.* I pull the curtain closed and reach toward a more realistic option. It's hard to stifle the laugh that wants to acknowledge Gavin's reaction, but I manage.

This one is sexy, but not skimpy like the last one—and actually provides butt coverage. It's navy blue and pretty standard as far as bikinis go. I like it, so I don't bother to model it for the guys. When I step out fully dressed, they are still standing in the same spot.

"Tell me you decided on the black one," the owner says as he slaps Gavin on the back of the shoulder. Gavin doesn't respond beyond looking at the guy like he might punch him, depending on what comes out of his mouth next. Then he reaches out for me to take his hand. The gesture is surprisingly sweet and catches me off guard because I'm still not used to this side of him.

At the counter, Gavin asks, "Which ones do you like better?" then puts on each of the sunglasses he put aside while I was trying stuff on. They are so similar, it hardly matters—plus, they both look sexy as hell.

"The first ones," I decide as I hand the owner my choice in swimsuit. If he is disappointed in my decision, he keeps it to himself. Gavin hands him the sunglasses and then inserts his card before I can pull my own out of my wallet. When I look at him kind of stunned, he just smiles. I don't know about the sunglasses or swim trunks, but my suit was a hundred and seventy dollars.

**

When we sit down at an outdoor café a few blocks from the surf shop, I lean toward him over the table and say, "Thank you for the swimsuit."

"My pleasure, Alabama. And thank *you* for not choosing the black one," he says as he relaxes back into his seat.

"You didn't like it?" I tease.

"No, I liked it a lot. What I didn't like was the chub you gave Smiley." He says this as he gestures over his shoulder in the direction of the store and also in full hearing range of the waiter who has just approached our table.

We order our lunch, and as soon as we are alone again, I feel the need to clear the air. After our kiss-fest last night, I don't want anything left unsaid to linger.

"Gavin, you are one of the sexiest men I have ever seen. I'm sorry I made you feel anything different than that." He pauses for a second, reflecting on what I've just said, and then sits forward.

"Ok."

"That's it? Just ok?"

"Yeah, for now."

"Does that mean you aren't done punishing me for it?"

"I haven't decided yet."

The server disrupts our conversation by setting our drinks down in front of us and saying our lunch will be right out. It's nice because it saves me from having to respond to Gavin's cryptic answer. Perhaps we are not past the punishment phase, after all.

"Gavin, tell the truth. Does a part of you still hate me?" I ask. I need to know if the kissing was partly for revenge. It would be vicious retribution for me to fall for him now, only to have him discard me. It would be cruel, but I have to at least entertain the thought. Last night didn't feel insincere—like, at all. However, it would crush me to find out he sacrificed that battle in order to win the war.

He widens his eyes slightly, perhaps caught off guard by my question. Then, he gives me a wolfish grin and shakes his head meticulously slow. Good, he doesn't hate me anymore. His demeanor does have a feral edge to it, however. It looks like he wants to drag me home by my hair and penetrate me in a multitude of different ways.

After a few seconds of feeling the weight of his gaze, he surprises me with his own question.

"Truth. Do my tattoos still bother you? You seem to be particularly agreeable in the dark." His stare is still heavy, maybe even accusatory. My jaw pops open like it's on a hinge. How can he even wonder about that at this point? I just told him he is one of the sexiest men I've ever seen. Which wires got crossed exactly? That wound must be deep if he is still holding so tightly to such a conviction.

I clear my throat, move my iced tea to the side, and lean in. He needs to hear this loud and clear. "Yes, they do." Now *he* leans in on his forearms. He's interpreted those words as an act of war.

There is a cyclone brewing in his eyes. A violent, dangerous one. His eyes always convey so much of what he is feeling. Right now, they are telling me how much he hates that he allowed himself to be vulnerable last night. How he should have known better. And now he's gearing up for a brawl.

"Do you want to know what bothers me about them? Here goes. I hate that I don't know if they make your skin more or less sensitive beneath my fingernails. It bothers me that I don't know what they feel like against my tongue, or if they taste as rugged and sexy as they look. It also bugs me that I don't know the meaning behind the cow skull, the Viking, the smoking revolvers—or any of the rest of them. And I hate that I don't know what they feel like between my teeth."

He is frozen, like there's a delay between what I've just said, and what he absorbs. His eyes are still a little hostile, but peace is approaching from beyond the frayed horizon.

"And I *really* hate that you still think I'm that person," I exclaim. This is the part that bothers me the most. It's deep-seated, the idea of perception vs. reality. I wear people's impressions of me like shackles. The adoration or disdain for my father naturally coated me as well. There was no way to defend myself against the negative perceptions, no way to address the masses, so they expected perfection of me. No missteps along the way were tolerated, but the thing is, no one can live up to the expectation of perfection.

I loathe the fact that Gavin has put such little stock in the countless good things I've done and said, yet still clings to the one horrible thing. He chooses to ignore reality in favor of the perception held so tightly in his grip.

"I don't."

"You don't what?" Now I'm confused. I was pretty deep in my mental indignation, so now I have to realign myself with the current conversation.

"I don't still think you're that person."

"When did you decide that?" I ask, now that my anger is starting to diffuse, I'd like to know.

"When I watched you teach that veteran the Cotton-Eyed Joe, probably. Or maybe when you danced with everyone who asked, so you wouldn't hurt their feelings. I don't know—somewhere in there."

"Then why did you ask if I have a problem with your tattoos?"

"Because you can still be a good person, and not like tattoos," his answer skewers me because it's obvious he no longer thinks I'm a horrible snob, but it's just as obvious that he's still worried he's not my type.

"Gavin. I want to rub my naked body all over your tattoos. I want to feel how soft they are against my skin. I want to trace each one of them with my tongue. And I want to do naughty things to you while you use your tattoo machine on someone. Ok?"

He smiles, "As long as we are being honest, I've wanted to suck on that bottom lip since you first started talking," then he leans forward to do just that.

***

In stark contrast to last night, the pool deck is reasonably crowded, and the hot tub is bubbling away and full of people. I head straight for the one empty cabana while Gavin peels off toward the bar. His muscled back and tattooed arms garner a fair amount of attention, but what has me panting, is the way his swim trunks hang. He looks delicious in clothes—but out of them, *just, wow.*

It's no damn wonder why he had such a hard time with my rejection. I bet he's never been anything but praised, and certainly, no one has ever accused him of not being their type. Nope, not this one. His demeanor in the crowd is similar to his attitude about tattooing—he likes being the best, he just doesn't like to announce it. But trust me, his hot body announces it just fine.

The rest of our lunch conversation had been light, if not dismissive of my direct mention of our turbulent past. I figure he wants to avoid such talk, either because he is a dude and doesn't like to talk about feelings, or because he hasn't processed his emotions about me yet.

Granted, last night hit as if by storm, so attempting to slow the momentum long enough to stop and think about what was going on was never going to happen. Everything was much simpler in the dark. Past grievances faded into the shadows, feelings weren't trampled on in order to gain the upper hand, sharp words had dulled into something else. Now, in the daylight, it's time to clear up anything that still might be blurry for him.

I'm just finishing applying my sunscreen when Gavin enters with two drinks. He looks around for somewhere to put the plastic cups, but besides a double style cabana bed, there is nothing else in here. He shrugs and gives me a *let's go* gesture with his head.

Once in the water, it's mere seconds before Gavin backs me into the corner and deposits our drinks on the edge of the pool by each of my shoulders. When he doesn't back up, I move my gaze from the beads of water glistening on his chest up to his new sunglasses.

"Do you want to know why I had a problem with the black bikini?" he asks, and because he is taller and also looking down at me, I feel like he's admonishing me like a naughty child. I nod.

"It's because I could see *exactly* what you look like naked," he leans down to my ear and repeats, "*exactly.*"

"Why was that a problem for you?" I ask.

"Because every other guy would see you like that too. We could vividly see the shape and hardness of your nipples. And we could tell that your pussy is bare," he says as he steps a little closer and runs the knuckles of his index finger back and forth across said area.

"You couldn't *see* that, you just know it is," I challenge. Even thinking about his fingers on that part of my body last night makes my whole face feel warm, and it has nothing to do with the sun.

He slowly shakes his head and lowers his voice, "Smiley at the surf shop knows *precisely* what your naked body looks like. He is going to think about it tonight when he jerks off." He is teasing me, not as blatantly as he normally would, but teasing just the same.

I lean forward, so my lips lightly graze against the hollow of his throat when I ask, "What do *you* think about when you jerk off?" I ask, wanting to know if he'll get uncomfortable when I turn the tables.

"All kinds of stuff."

"Like what? What did you think about last night in the shower?"

"Are you sure you're ready for this conversation? Because I have all sorts of filthy images and impure thoughts in my head."

"Were you thinking about how it felt to have your fingers in my panties?" I ask. Now, my lips are less of a graze, and more of a kiss—same spot. His mouth drifts down to my ear, and when he talks, his words rumble in my chest.

"No. Last night I was thinking about fucking your mouth, eating you out, and fingering your ass, all at the same time." He raises his eyebrows unapologetically while I furrow my brow and try to work that out in my head.

"Don't think too hard about that one. I'm not talking circus freak stuff—just your standard sixty-nine. Oh, and you were *amazing*, by the way," he leans in closer, and I see that he is pinching his mouth shut so he doesn't laugh outright.

"*Those* are your filthy and impure thoughts?" I ask, "Just your standard, sixty-nine?" All I'm doing now is trying to keep up with him. His dirty talk always makes me squirm—which, is no doubt why he employs such tactics. But after last night, there are quite a bit of filthy thoughts swirling around in my own head.

No one is paying an ounce of attention to us tucked away in the corner of the pool like this, but it still doesn't feel wholly appropriate to be discussing his impure thoughts out in the open like this.

Now he does laugh outright, "No, Alabama. Not even close." He stops me from asking just how dirty his thoughts get with his mouth on mine.

By the time he pulls back from our kiss, all the ice has melted in our drinks, so they taste like watered down Kool-Aid. It doesn't matter, though, because the *last* thing I'm thinking about is hydration.

"Wrap your legs around my waist," Gavin commands, and when I do, he steps into me and starts kissing my neck. There are no kids out here, but still, this is highly inappropriate in a hotel pool.

"Let's get out of the water," I suggest, at the same time melting against his talented mouth. He loops his arms around my lower back, holding me in place, and all of a sudden, I don't care what anyone thinks.

"Good idea, come on," he says as he lowers me down and takes my hand to lead me to the steps and out of the pool.

I'm not entirely sure the cabana is much better for privacy. We have the one furthest from the pool and bar but are still very much a part of the music and festivities.

"Much better," he says as he flops down on the wide chaise lounge. "If my dick got any harder, I would have been stuck in the pool for a while." He taps the spot next to him and says, "Come rub your body up against my tattoos."

I laugh because he hadn't said much when I told him I wanted to do that with my *naked* body, but evidently, it registered for him. I crawl toward him, wishing we were back in the room instead of at the rooftop pool. "It won't have the same effect if I'm wearing a swimsuit," I counter, as I lie down next to him.

"Ok, then, come tell me what you were like as a kid instead."

***

We talk for a long time about everything and nothing at all, and it has never been clearer how right my friends were. He has more passion for life in his left nut than the last five guys I've dated combined. He is ambitious, but not the kind that steps on people's necks to get ahead—those are the ones I usually pick for myself.

We are lying down on our sides, facing each other. Our bodies mirror one another in how we both rest our heads against a propped-up hand. He tells me all about the childhood art teacher that recognized his artistic talent and bought him his first figure drawing book—then he seamlessly moves his free hand from my waist and thumbs my nipple through the damp bathing suit.

His touch has an immediate role in vacating my brain of our previous conversation. The focused attention on my nipple sits heavy as a brick between my legs, and my lips part, but I find I have nothing to say.

"Tell me about your friends," he prompts, as if he has nothing to do with the erotic vibration humming through all my bodily functions.

"What?" I breathe as he slips the triangle of fabric off my breast with one skilled swipe of his thumb. He closes some of the gap between us, and his lips make contact with mine at the same time he tugs on my nipple.

"Your friends," he says against my gasp. "They chose me for you...why?" he asks in the flicker of time our lips part. He's already working the swimsuit top off my other breast as if we were not in an open-walled cabana with twenty other people nearby.

When he moves his face back from mine and rests it again on his bicep so I can answer the question, I try to tighten up some of the space that separates us, so I don't feel so exposed. My bikini top now does nothing but frame my half-naked display. In truth, no one can see my chest, but I'm very aware of the buzz of people around us, so I *feel* every bit of my unveiling.

He places his palm against my sternum to stop me from inching forward. "Let me look at you," he says with a husky scratch to his voice.

"But everybody—"

"No one else can see you." His free hand fondles its way over and then cups my breast.

"Let me see your body," he repeats the sentiment, then his gaze strays from my eyes. Between the heat of his stare and his decisive fingers, he has my nipples standing at full attention and my brain too foggy to answer his question about my friends.

"Your friends," he prompts.

"Uhhhh. Ok. You met Miles and Ivy, and then there is Arden. She is pretty consumed by her boyfriend, so we only see her for happy hour here and there."

"Do you know what I find curious about your friends?" he asks. He is back to looking me in the eyes while we talk, but his fingers are hardly idle.

"What?" I ask, there is absolutely nothing wrong with my friends, so I'd like to see where he goes with this.

"We just spent an hour talking about your parents and how judgmental and intolerant they are of everyone."

"And?" I ask, not really sure what my narrow-minded parents have to do with anything. Before, I was trying to explain my snap decision about his unsuitability because of his tattoos and piercings.

"Do you really not see where I'm going with this?" he asks with humor in his tone.

"My parents are narrow-minded assholes. My friends are the best things that ever happened to me," I say emphatically. My mom and dad don't even belong in the same sentence as my friends. Where is he going with this?

The smile that splits his face is contagious as he brings his hand over my waist, so he can pull me closer and drag his fingers back and forth across a bare spot on my back.

"Your parents are intolerant bigots, and one of your best friends is gay, and one of them is black."

"I've only seen my parents a couple of times a year, for the last eight years. I don't give two shits what they think about Miles and Ivy, and I'm *most certainly* not friends with them to prove something to my ignorant parents." I've got to be honest, I'm pretty fired up right now about what he is insinuating. "I don't care what they look like or how they identify. I'm friends with those two because they are fucking awesome."

"Hey," he kisses my lips, then says, "I agree with you. I'm not saying that's *why* you are friends with them." Another kiss, "I'm pointing out how amazing it is that you are nothing like your parents." He must realize the tide shift because he adjusts my top back to where it belongs.

"Oh."

"And that gives me some perspective because I spent a fair amount of time angry at that part of you. Keep in mind, I spent all this time getting to know you online and thinking you were a certain way, and when we met, you were nothing like I thought. I was angry and disappointed. Actually, I was angry *because* I was disappointed. I have all sorts of drawings that speak to those feelings."

"I get it, but first of all, my friends know me better than I know myself—just because it was them online instead of me doesn't mean you got bad information. Second of all, if you ever want to see what white-hot rage looks like, tell me I'm just like my parents. Unfortunately, I made a snap judgment about you, and then I verbalized it. That doesn't make me narrow-minded or intolerant of people's differences or *anything* like my parents. It makes me human. People make snap judgements every day. You do it too. Now, *obviously,* we need to talk about these drawings you just referenced."

"Wait a sec. I'll get to the drawings, but first I need to clarify something. I don't make snap judgments about people."

"Liar," I crack a smile, "You judge people who get sorority letter tattoos and tramp stamps. You said people who go overboard with body modifications are insecure. You said that woman with the crazy fingernails had daddy issues because her boyfriend was so much older than her. You said Sam the bartender was a rapist. And tell me, why didn't you sleep with that fuel girl who was humping your leg? Was she too slutty for you? Hmmm? Not your type?"

"No. I didn't sleep with her because I had my mind on someone else." He pulls me against him and nuzzles my ear, "Plus, Sam probably is a rapist." His muffled voice in my ear canal incites a riot of goosebumps down the left side of my body.

"That's my point. There are two types of people in the world, those who judge people without knowing them…and liars." He coughs out a laugh, but he knows I'm right. "Now that we've established that you are no different than me, let's talk about those angry drawings."

He rolls away so that he's lying on his back, and lets out a big sigh while I make sure he did a decent job of fixing my top. "What do you want me to say? Art is my outlet."

"Go on."

"They are not all bad, some of them are really hot." He looks very self-conscious, and I know he is not used to defending his craft.

"When you say *bad*, do you mean like really bad? Like I'm dead or beat-up or something?"

"No. Nothing like that. Just like, angry fucking—not like, hurting you or against your will or anything, just…rougher than I would normally be, and more disrespectful than I would ever be. Jesus, I sound like a psychopath."

"Rough, how?"

"Choking, hair pulling, gagging you with my cock—"

"Disrespectful, how?"

"Just, like…tit fucking you and coming all over your face—Please keep in mind that before this conversation, you wanted to know my filthy thoughts. I mean…the drawings are dirty, and they involve a lot of cum dripping off your tits and ass, but they're not deranged or anything. They aren't of you tied up or helpless in any way—Scratch that, there are a couple of you tied up, but those are some of the sexy drawings, not the angry ones."

"Alright, let's talk about the sexy ones then," I say. For some reason, I'm not bothered by the angry drawings, especially because he is so candid about them. I get that drawing is his outlet. And I would be remiss in leaving out the fact that I've had guys do some of that stuff to me and think nothing of it. At least Gavin recognizes when it's disrespectful, or not the *fun* type of rough.

"I told you, they're hot. I've got a healthy imagination, and I'm pretty good at drawing." He flashes a sexy wink at me that works like a magnet because I lean over him and plant a kiss that was meant to be brief but turns into something else entirely.

"I'd rather show you than tell you about them," he mumbles into our kiss. I pull back, a little surprised that he would show them to me. I figured it would be like letting someone read your journal—private and intensely personal.

"You would show me those drawings?" I ask, wide-eyed, but completely touched. He gives me that slow head shake and primal grin he has perfected, and I realize that's not at all what he meant about showing me. Now, my heart beats faster, and I'm all done at the pool.

Chapter 22

When we get back to the room, the first thing I want to do is take a shower and wash off all the sweat and sunscreen. The first thing he wants to do is fill two glasses with ice water and pound them both. Then, he refills one and hands it to me, which is sweet.

"I'm going to take a quick shower," I say because it's about to get sexy in here, and I don't want to be all sweaty and gross when it goes down.

"I have a better idea," he says, so I stop and turn around. "How about you take a bath instead…and I'll get my sketchbook?"

"Hotel bathtubs aren't all that sexy, Gavin…or clean."

"It will be perfect. We'll throw some bubbles in there…get you all clean," the words break off with his mischievous smile, and I can tell he is not at all worried about the state of the tub's cleanliness. It looks like I'm taking a bath.

While the tub fills and Gavin gets his stuff together for our flight home tonight, I wind my hair up into something wild and unruly on top of my head. Then, naturally, I touch up my makeup and apply lip gloss— because that's what everyone does before a bath.

I'm still standing in the bathroom in my bikini, with a toothbrush in my mouth, when Gavin rounds the corner and places his sketchbook and a pencil on the bathroom counter. He stands behind me and puts both hands on my hips. Then, while watching me through the tops of his eyes in the mirror, he begins kissing my neck.

All of a sudden, I'm less concerned with the bright light and lack of scented candles for my bath. When I bend forward to spit toothpaste

159

into the sink, he backs up a fraction. I think, to keep a respectful distance between my ass and his dick.

When I finish brushing my teeth and straighten up, he lightly brushes the hair at the base of my neck aside. Then, he follows up with a kiss that tickles so much, my nipples harden into something ferocious. The fact that he watches our reflection in the mirror makes the whole thing even hotter.

When the top tie of my bikini unfastens and the whole thing flops forward, I'm impressed by how stealthily he accomplished such a feat. But even that feeling is eclipsed by the one I get when his hands come up to cup and play with my breasts.

"*Jesus,*" he breathes into the side of my neck before resting his forehead on my shoulder to compose himself. I take it he's a boob-man. He moves his mouth to my ear and murmurs, "Maybe you should skip the bath," while he rolls my nipples roughly between his fingers and thumbs.

"Maybe you should join me," I suggest as my head lolls back. All my attention is on his tugging fingers. I can't even focus on supporting my head right now.

"Not today," he says.

After a few gratuitous minutes, I step away from him to pour the hotel body wash into the stream of surging water flowing from the faucet. Gavin scoots back on the counter and then leans against the wall, paper and pencil at the ready.

"I need to get something down on paper, this is too perfect not to capture. I know it seems weird, but I draw from my imagination, or I copy a photo someone gives me. I never have a real live model as a reference." He glances away shyly, then looks back at me and says, "You have to embrace the artist in me—even when it seems strange or involves incredibly bad timing."

I smile at him as I pull the strap at my right hip, untying that side. "I don't think it's strange at all." His eyes immediately drop to my mid-section, so I untie the left side and let the bottoms drop to the floor. Now, I am completely naked, and lit up like a violin soloist with this horrible lighting. I'd say I am intensely uncomfortable under his close scrutiny, but he is enraptured, so I stand here a few seconds longer instead of diving under the bubbles to hide my imperfect nakedness.

I turn off the faucet and step in. Now, I'm going to be honest here, and admit that my first thought is not about the dead-sexy man watching me right now, it's that I hope I don't get a UTI from the one-two punch of the bubbles and the lingering bacteria in the dirty tub. However, that thought is quickly blurred as I lie back because the water is so hot it prickles my skin and feels almost cold.

"Is it too hot or too cold?" he asks in recognition of the pained look on my face.

"Too hot," I exclaim as I quickly sit forward. Gavin, problem solver that he is, goes and gets the ice bucket.

"Some, or all of it?" he asks, then says, "Never mind," as he dumps the whole thing in. The coolness hits my stomach all at once, then spreads like smoky tendrils down my limbs. It's an instant relief, and I feel better right away, so I'm able to lie back again.

He reassumes his position next to the sink, and for a bit, he just stares at me. Then he tucks his head and begins sketching. I'd say he applies himself for about three and a half minutes, looks up again—a few seconds past awkward, then down again for maybe two minutes. After that, he hops off the counter and drops his swim trunks.

The tub is small and narrow, so it takes some commitment on both of our parts to finally get situated. Not to mention, the image of his half-hard dick is burned on the backs of my eyelids and has significantly slowed my response time.

"Did you ever spider swing with anyone when you were a kid?" I ask, because minus the swing set and chains to hold on to, that's precisely what we are doing. He laughs and pulls me forward, so my naked parts touch his naked parts. My gasp is hidden by his response.

"Yes, I did. I was much smaller than her, though, so I was on top. You know, when that first came out of my mouth it sounded a little emasculating, but as I think it through, it's not at all. Because I was with my babysitter," he waggles his eyebrows at me and then places a soapy palm on my jaw to guide me closer to his snickering mouth.

The kiss is pretty innocent—more of a preliminary round before the crazy one hits, but the fact that my vagina is snug up against the bottom side of his erection, shadows his intent a bit. It brings the innocence of the kiss to the next level, which is borderline raunchy.

I am trying not to rub up against him, but it's really hard because of the way he holds and leisurely kisses me. It's slow and passionate—reverent even.

He disengages his mouth but at the same time rests his forehead against mine, so the valley between us remains narrow. His hand still cradles my cheek, and for a few beats, all he does is breathe. I get the impression he is trying to slow things down.

"There's something I have wanted to tell you for a long time, Alabama. I can't even fully enjoy your body or your mouth until I get it off my chest." I pull back from him. This doesn't sound good.

"Is this when you tell me you are *married?*" I ask with so much derision in my voice, it doesn't even sound like my own.

He looks stunned, like I just slapped him with a dead salmon. If he's married, I will get out of this tub and be out of this room within three minutes.

"No! I'm not married. Fucking hell, what do you take me for?" Now both of his hands are holding my face. "*No*, it's nothing like that," he says gently.

"What then? Just say it." My chest feels like it's been caved in by all the disappointment hanging in the air. Why is trust such a fickle bitch? He lightly kisses my lips, but the only thing I return is an empty stare.

"I want to tell you, I'm sorry I called you a *cunt*. It was completely unacceptable, and I'm ashamed of myself for saying it."

It takes some time to register what he just said, but then I risk a smile at his acknowledgment. I've often wondered if he remembered saying such a thing.

"That's not who I am. I wanted to kick my own ass after I said it." He looks completely sincere and dangerously sexy—more so now because of his admission and apology.

"And I'd also like to say that it made me really proud of you to hear you stand up for yourself after I said it."

"Yeah? Well, no one has ever called me a cunt before. I'm glad my instinct was to defend myself."

"Somehow, I doubt you've ever *not* stood up for yourself," he laughs. This time when he wraps his arms around my lower back to secure me against him, one hand drifts down between my cheeks. Though his fingers dally, he doesn't penetrate me. It's more like he is feeling out my comfort level. He is playing, not entering.

Come to think of it, last night when he got me off, he didn't press his fingers inside of me either. It seems purposeful now that I analyze his lack of penetration, and Ivy's words rise to the surface of my mind, *he never would have had sex with you after just one date.*

I'm done pondering his fingers and their apparent boundaries because while the fingers of one hand play, his other hand flattens against the sway of my back and pulls me tightly against his prominent erection. At this point, I don't know who's motion is grinding us together, but the sensation halts my breath and steals my thoughts.

"You feel incredible, *Alabama*," he grinds out all raspy, like he just smoked a pack of cigarettes. "Are you done with your bath? Because I'm ready to find out what you taste like."

I grab a towel on the way out of the bathroom, but Gavin thwarts my efforts to wrap it around myself by hoisting me up to his hips and attacking my mouth. We are still wet, and perhaps a little soapy, so when I wrap my legs around his waist, our skin feels slick and overheated.

He has one arm holding me against him while he somewhat crawls up the bed, depositing me somewhere near the middle of it.

"I'm not going to fuck you right now because I don't want to skip the natural progression of our relationship—or have sex with you for the first time in a hotel room—but, Alabama?"

"*What?*" I ask while literally squirming beneath his water dappled body, and his heavy erection sways above me.

"I'm still going to have you howling from the most intense orgasms you've ever had, and if your throat isn't raw from screaming my name, it will be because I'm not done yet." Then his mouth is on my neck, my hands are in his hair, and our bodies writhe together against a craving that must rival a heroin addiction.

He kisses his way down my cleavage and then aggressively pinches one nipple while simultaneously teasing the other one gently with his tongue.

"Which one?" he asks, still tonguing my nipple while looking up at my face. I shudder involuntarily against the erotic mutiny taking place within. When I don't answer right away, he gives another rough pinch along with the paradoxical ticklish flutter.

"Both," I groan as I squeeze my hands into fists, tugging his hair in the process. I can't choose between a light or rough touch, they both seem essential to me. Each of my nipples hum from the diverse attention—but in very different ways.

"Good girl," he says wickedly before he reverses his method. I'm going out of my mind while he unravels my body. The use of his tongue piercing is calculated and very deliberate—and he engages it at will. It's far enough back on his tongue that it doesn't get in the way of kissing, but it's also far enough forward to offer a startling array of new and wonderful sensations.

When he starts to nibble on my hip and creep his hand between my thighs, he can tell that my legs are already shaking. It might be a mixture of the cold air and my neediness, but it's not cold in here at all. He slides his palm up the inside of my thigh, from my knee straight to the heat of my vagina. His hand is warm and inquisitive, then he widens his fingers, spreading me apart.

"You are so completely sexy, I don't even know where to start," he says as he grins up at me. He must only see a look of delirium on my face because between last night, the cabana, and the bathtub—I have never been so wound up or needed someone so bad. Add to that the fact that he's already said we're not having sex, and I feel like a grenade that had its pin pulled fifteen minutes ago.

"Spread your legs, I want to see you."

I hesitate because it seems crude and indecent. But he must disagree because he adds, "Nice and wide, Alabama, I've been thinking about this moment for a long time."

"You have?" I ask, touched—however ridiculous that sounds.

"I've busted a lot of nut thinking about your tight little pussy. So, now, I want to look at it." He sits back on his knees, between my legs as I widen them. I feel shy doing it, but also naughty, and like I have some unchecked power over him.

"*Jesus, Alabama,*" his voice is scratched apart. It's like he sees some sort of revelation and feels spiritually moved by it. He looks at me far longer than is entirely polite, which only serves to intensify the heat of my embarrassment. Then he lowers his face to the altar and begins to pray.

Chapter 23

When his mouth first makes contact with my revealing display, he moans the sexiest sound of satisfaction I've ever heard. It kind of mirrors my own. But when I feel the warm silver ball of his piercing swipe up my crease, opening me for the tip of his tongue, I reflexively jerk away from his mouth and the rapid onslaught of sensation.

He is undaunted, in fact, he may even up his efforts because then he gently sucks my clit with his warm satiny mouth. Then, when blood has rushed the area, he runs the metal ball back and forth over it. Just that sequence alone is enough to make me come if he repeated it a few more times. But I get the impression he is in it for the marathon, not the sprint.

"*Gavin,*" I whisper pant, "*It's so good, oh my God, it's so good,*" I can't lie still, and arching my back changes his angle—but I can't help it, my neck strains back, my hands clutch the pillows behind me—and I'm about to come—already.

When it happens, I grind my teeth together trying to offset the intensity of it. So, a long, drawn-out, growly sound is what accompanies the wild pulsing of my body.

Gavin rides out my orgasm with one hand flat on my stomach and the other arm looped under my thigh and holding it open. He eases up on his ministrations almost completely during my climax, but he doesn't stop. Not at all.

After only a couple of minutes of lighter, post-orgasm flicks with his tongue, my legs really start to shake. He slides one hand heavily up my torso and begins to roll my nipple between his fingers. Then he releases his hold on my thigh and brings that hand down to where his mouth meets my body. He widens two fingers into the shape of a V, further opening me for the rumble of the metal ball that sits wickedly on his tongue.

Mere seconds go by before I moan that I'm about to come again. He evidently finds that humorous because I can feel his chuckle with remarkable clarity. This time, he leaves my sensitive clit alone while I shiver from the inside out, but he still rubs his piercing against the raw part of my body exposed between his widened fingers.

I'm not a screamer when I climax—I'm more of an internal rejoicer, so no one is more surprised than me when I shout, *"Fuuuuck! Gavin! Ahhhhhh-fuck-gahhhh!"* with my latest orgasm.

When it's over, he crawls up my body—arrogant grin firmly in place, and whispers in my ear, *"I'm just getting started,"* and then he kisses a trail of self-satisfaction up my jawline to my mouth.

I'm not saying he shouldn't be proud of himself, I just got off twice—in record time, but he wears his cockiness like a cape. Actually, you know what? He earned that swagger. Some guys don't know a clitoris from a pound cake, much less what to do with one. Gavin—he, gets the gold and silver medals.

My whole body is humming. Like, actually vibrating when I bring my hands up to hold his face for a long, indulgent kiss. Then the phone rings, and the jarring sound startles us both.

Lifting his head, and still drunk from our kiss, Gavin grabs the pillow that's partially under my head and chucks it at the phone. Effectively silencing the ringing by knocking the thing to the floor. Then he resumes tugging my bottom lip between his teeth.

I reach down to stroke him, having every intention of returning the favor. It's hot and stiff as a post. When I touch it, he leans his forehead against mine. "I'm not finished with you yet. I was just giving you a few minutes to recover. So, stay—just like this," he says.

I'm not comfortable with our union being so one-sided. And the fantasy he told me about earlier has just jumped to the forefront of my mind. *I was fucking your mouth.*

"Ok. I'll stay just like this..." I stroke him a few more times before I continue, "...If you kneel above me—*and fuck my mouth.*"

He doesn't respond, he just closes his eyes and breathes against whatever is racing through his head right now. Slowly, he opens his eyes, pupils blown, and says, "What are you trying to do to me?" Then he drops his head and laughs. "I almost just came in your hand."

Then I laugh too because I know he is kidding, but the thought is still really funny. Gavin, popping off like a fifteen-year-old in my hand because I talked a little dirty to him.

"I'm not really sure how to say no to that, Alabama," he is shaking his head, but the laughter is still on his lips.

"Good because now, *I'm* just getting started," I toss his words right back at him, and he rolls off of me onto his back, possibly realizing he has met his match.

With Gavin's arm draped over his eyes and his straining erection swaying like a divining rod, I grab two of the non-thrown pillows and adjust them beneath my neck and shoulders.

He apparently comes to terms with the change of events and situates himself so that he kneels above my hips. He hesitates, and I'm not sure why. It's either because he's worried 'fucking my mouth' will come across as disrespectful, or he's worried it's too soon—kinda like the sex he's taken off the table.

I reach out and take his indecision in my hand, and when I rub the bottom side of it right at the base of his head, he comes to a rather quick decision. He eases forward, holding the base of his shaft. When he gets close enough, I lewdly hold out my tongue for him.

He slaps the head against my tongue twice in quick succession but doesn't ease himself forward yet. So, I use the tip of my tongue to tickle his sensitive frenulum, hoping to coax him forward.

He has one arm resting on top of the headboard and the other hand still wrapped around himself. Right now, he is on one knee, and the other foot is next to my shoulder. I think that position gives him more control, and he may be worried he'll be too much for me after fantasizing about this for so long.

In his mind, he could go as hard and fast and deep as he wanted to, but now I'm a real person, not a fantasy—and I think he's worried about crossing the line—or maybe about not recognizing the line once he gets going. Either way, he hesitates.

"Slide it in my mouth, Gavin."

He drops his head back in defeat, but he does advance—slowly. I do what I can to rise up to meet him and flick and swirl my tongue around the tip. As he progresses forward a bit more, I begin to suck, which loosens him up enough to start carefully pumping in and out.

He still keeps his movement very shallow, so I moan with encouragement. Which works like a charm, and he begins to lengthen his stride. My arms are between his legs, and bracing him from behind, so I can also reassure him by encouraging his thrust.

He's a big guy, so there is no chance of deep throating him or even taking him to the back of my throat without my molars causing problems, but I still have every confidence that this blow job will leave him with a lasting impression.

I've created an abundance of saliva, which is intensely satisfying for him to have the slip along with the suction. It's also quite provocative that we've maintained eye contact the whole time. Then, all of a sudden, someone is pounding on the door.

"What the fuck!" Gavin shouts as he withdraws himself from my mouth and looks over in the direction of the door. Then he shoots me a panicked look, "Alabama, what time is it?"

Chapter 24

I've never almost missed a flight before, but the fact that we are on this plane right now is a testament to our speeding Uber driver and some lenient TSA agents. The flight attendants actually had to re-open the door of the plane as we ran down the access ramp.

Thankfully, the impatient hotel staff had taken exception to the fact we hadn't checked out yet, and housekeeping needed to get in to clean the room for the next guests.

I'd say the whole, almost missing our flight thing, was due to being so caught up in each other, but in our defense, our internal clocks were all jacked up after sleeping in so late. If you would have asked me, I'd have said we had another two hours before we needed to get to the airport.

Anyway, we made it. And after our walk of shame down the narrow aisle, where everyone we passed treated us to a scowly look, we find our seats in the back of the plane. That's what happens when you hold up a flight. They save you a spot right outside of the bathroom.

The other seat on our side of the aisle is thankfully empty, and on the other side is an elderly couple and their own empty seat.

"What does the rest of your week look like?" Gavin asks as the plane starts to pick up speed down the runway.

"I have to work. I need to salvage a huge account that I fumbled so I could come here." I raise the armrest, so I can turn and face him better. He looks like he's got something brewing upstairs, but when he looks at me, he doesn't immediately say anything.

"What about you? Long hours leaving your mark across America?" He furrows his brows and faces me pointedly. "I'm teasing. You didn't just take offense to that, did you? You are a tattoo artist, you leave your mark."

Ignoring my comment, he asks, "What do you mean, *salvage a huge account that you fumbled so you could come here?*" The way he has closed in on me, pinning me between the isle and his inquisition, makes me feel a little reprimanded.

"It's nothing—work is just busy, and I'm responsible for some of the bigger accounts these days. That's all." I try to minimize the impact of my last loud-mouth statement. I don't want him to get all high and mighty on me right now. I'm a grown woman. I can make decisions without his input or his approval.

"Uh Huh," he says, his voice void of any inflection whatsoever, as if he knows every word that just came out of my lips was a dirty, foul-mouthed lie.

"Now, why don't you try telling me the truth, Alabama? You act like I haven't been paying attention. I know damn well you just got promoted and are in charge of all the exclusivity contracts. I also know you outperformed your peers eight of the last twelve months. That doesn't sound like someone who fumbles anything." His stare is accusatory, and maybe a little hurt.

If you want the truth, I'm impressed he remembered all that from our coffee date. I don't remember one detail of anything he talked about that day. Well—other than, redheads aren't his type. That one kinda stuck with me.

"Ok, fine. I had a big client meeting on Friday, and I didn't handle re-scheduling it very well. I rushed it into Thursday evening, and I wasn't prepared for it."

"Are you sure it didn't go well?"

"It was pretty bad." At that, he drops his head back against the seat and exhales a long breath.

"Why did you do that? So you could come to help me, right?"

"Listen, I may lose that account, but it won't jeopardize my whole career. And for your information, salvaging my integrity was more important than landing that contract. I'm thinking of the big picture stuff, Gavin."

"Why was it so important to change my mind about you?"

"What do you mean? I couldn't stand that you thought I was that shitty of a person. You know—a cunt," I exaggerate that last part. To no avail, though, because he's undaunted and presses further.

"But why did you care what *I* thought?"

"Gavin, I care what everybody thinks. Especially if they think I am like my parents."

"Hold on, quick detour here. You have to let that go, you know that, right? You are not your parents, fine. So, get the hell out of their shadow." His statement hits me hard. It resonates some, but it's really harsh coming out of his mouth.

I want to tell him I'll never be able to get out from their shadow because it's sewn on to me somehow, just like my green eyes and the double chin that's inevitably coming down the pipes, but I can't get the words out. I nod in acknowledgment because I know he is right. I also don't want to keep talking about it, so I leave my response at the nod.

"Is there anything I can do?" he asks as he takes my hand. He probably can sense that I'm shutting down. Between my misstep at work and my parents, this conversation is going nowhere good.

"No, because it's too late to adopt me," I try using humor, but it doesn't really deflect anything.

"I mean to help salvage your big account?"

"Let's just see where the shit lands, and go from there," I say. The truth is, I've avoided everything that has to do with work. I haven't so much as checked my email, let alone followed up with the bobbled client.

"It's going to be weird acclimating to our real lives again. I'm not sure how I'm going to kiss you goodbye and then only see you here and there when we have time," he says.

His words sit like hot coals in my stomach, and I have no real response. The truth is that I'm going to miss him. I don't even know what type of relationship he wants with me. Are we talking once a week we see each other? Texts and little else? How do I go from 24/7 where we are now, to a few dates peppered into our busy lives? Is that all he wants?

He must read something into my silence because he tips my chin up so I meet his eyes. "We have spent just about every moment together for the past four days. I only mean we won't be together like that once we get home." His explanation immediately makes me feel better about the relationship he wants with me.

"Yeah, and just when I'm finally used to you showboating your morning wood."

"Right, and I'm finally accustomed to your odd choices in sleepwear and complete refusal to use a pillow."

I smile wistfully and lean my head on his shoulder. Being a late flight, the captain dimmed the lights, and that, coupled with the hum of the engines, should lull me to sleep or at least relax me. However, the surprisingly loud, open-mouthed breathing in the row next to us is rather distracting. The woman must be used to her husband's emphatic sleep habits, though, because she is conked out right next to him and sleeping soundly.

"Are you bummed the convention is over?" I ask.

"I won't miss working in all that chaos. I'm only bummed we left off where we did," he says with an unreadable smile on his lips. Does he mean, now that we are getting along? Or very specifically, with him receiving head? Before thinking better of it, I slide my palm up the inside of his thigh. He looks down at my hand and then back at my face.

"Do you mean, where we left off...here?" I ask as I flutter my fingers against the crotch of his jeans. I feel his penis twitch behind the denim, and it reminds me of the unrequited state of his desire.

"...or here?" I ask while tapping my lips with one finger.

He doesn't answer me. He just palms my ear and lands his mouth solidly against mine. When he pulls back a fraction, he says, "You can't possibly expect me to answer that." I flutter my fingers again and feel him start to stiffen against his thigh.

"You better stop. Things are about to get uncomfortable inside my jeans."

"Take off your sweatshirt," I tell him. He looks around before taking it off. I can see him calculate the risk, and then decide to take it. He drops the discarded clothing lightly on his lap while I unclasp his seatbelt and start popping open the buttons on his jeans.

After I get his fly open, I'm not really sure where to go from here. His half-hard dick is pretty trapped by the leg of his pants. Evidently, Gavin is used to such adjustments because he skillfully hoists the thing to freedom.

This turn of events is certainly a contrast from our flight *to* California, where he debated whether or not our seats should even be together, but a lot can happen in four days.

I loosen my own seatbelt to a ridiculous degree so I can turn toward him even more and also somewhat put my back to the aisle.

When I take his shaft in my hand, it feels unnaturally warm—kind of like me right now.

I assume a dry hand won't feel all that good, so I focus entirely on his glans. I may adjust my technique, but for now, just the head.

When I flicker the tip of my thumb against his frenulum, he closes his eyes and drops his head back against the seat. His skin feels like the softest satin, but he is bulging hard now that I've begun.

The process of an in-flight hand job is a little different because I really need to limit the amount of movement beneath his sweatshirt. The system that seems to work the best is wrapping my hand around him just beneath his coronal ridge and shallowly bumping over it. While my hand thumps up and back, my thumb alternates between swiping over his glans, and shimmying against his f-spot.

His breaths are starting to come faster, so it's no surprise when pre-cum oozes out and lubes up the whole process. By now, I've decided to mostly ignore his shaft and only employ a full stroke after nervously glancing around at my compromising surroundings.

It's quiet and seems like every passenger is engrossed in a book or movie or asleep—including the noisy sleepers across the aisle. Plus, not one single person has ventured to the back of the plane to use the restroom.

Gavin still has his head tipped back, but now and then, he will open his eyes, presumably to also assess our surroundings. The notable difference to his handsome face is the squared-off and bulging jaw that surfaced when he clenched his teeth. He hasn't made a sound, and that clench might be why.

Now, it's me who takes the calculated risk. I unclasp my loosened seatbelt entirely, scooch back as much as I can into the open seat, and move aside the sweatshirt.

Gavin opens his eyes when I remove the protective covering, but he doesn't fully lift his head until the tip of him is in my mouth. He tenses up for a few wild seconds while looking around, but he must come to the same conclusion I did about the other passengers because he relaxes into the seat again.

Cognizant of how it will look if I start bobbing up and down, I stick with my original plan. I turn my head so Gavin can see the side of my face, and then start rubbing the tip of my tongue against the sensitive spot on the underside of his head.

After many minutes of tonguing his f-spot, circling the ridge of his head, and occasionally sucking on the tip, Gavin squeezes his hand into a fist. This action serves two purposes. It aggressively pulls a handful of my hair, and it indicates the fact that he is about to come—which I'm already well aware of.

I close my mouth around him, bump my lips twice more over his coronal ridge, and then he comes violently in my mouth. I can feel his strain to keep quiet every bit as much as I can feel the ejaculate spurting from him. As much as I hate swallowing, there are not any other options short of him whitewashing the tray table in front of us.

After a couple of minutes, he finally loosens his grip on my hair. His eyes close again, and he tips his face toward the ceiling of the plane.

I attempt to put him back into his jeans, but he stops me by placing the wadded-up sweatshirt on his lap with one hand and helping me to sit up with the other. He still hasn't changed position or his expression, but he adjusts his arm so he can hold me snugly against his shoulder and chest.

I can feel this heart beating wildly beneath his shirt, and I can't help but feel a sense of pride. Gradually the pounding in his chest slows to a normal rhythm, and just when I think he must have fallen asleep, he tips his head and speaks into my hair.

"That was outstanding."

I wrap my unpinned arm around his abdomen and relax against him. I don't want this trip to end. Not ever. I don't want to go back to my empty loft and demanding career. I want to stay tucked against Gavin forever.

"Ballsy, but outstanding," he chuckles. I can feel the rumble of his laugh against my cheek. I should be laughing too, but I'm not. I'm way too busy thinking about the airport goodbye that's getting closer by the second. That, and wondering how long it will be before I can see him again.

Chapter 25

We walked through the airport hand in hand like an actual couple but had both been a little quiet. The late hour and long day on the horizon hadn't been the only reason for the somber tone. It seems we had both been anticipating our imminent goodbyes.

Gavin broke the silence with talk of logistics when he asked me if I parked or Ubered. Then, upon finding out we both parked in the economy lot, he walked me safely to my car.

Now we stand in the parking lot, and the dreaded moment is here. He leans against my driver's side door, preventing too hasty of a departure, as if that was really an issue.

"Come here," he says quietly, and then opens his arms for me to walk into them. When my face tucks into the crook of his neck, he hugs me tighter and then says, "Have dinner with me tomorrow night."

I answer him by kissing his neck, then migrating to his mouth for a surprisingly long, sensual kiss. After a while, he pulls his head back.

"Is that a, yes? I want to take you somewhere nice to thank you for helping me—at the risk of fire-bombing your pristine career path." His joking manner comes perhaps a little too soon for me to laugh about, so I answer simply.

"Yes."

"Good, now go home and get some sleep," he says, but instead of moving away from my door, he palms the back of my head and pulls me into another lengthy kiss.

When he finally decides it's time to go, he steps aside, opens the back door, and puts my suitcase in for me. Then he opens mine so I can get in.

"Goodnight, Alabama. Sweet dreams."

Chapter 26

Work is a shitshow, just as I anticipated it would be. It will take me a week to climb out from the rubble and get caught up. The old me would stay very late every night until I could flawlessly come out on top. That's the old me, though. The new me has a date with Gavin tonight.

The old me would probably wait until I got home this evening to return all of my friend's texts—but I'm not going to do that either. I can't concentrate on work anyway. I might as well use this time to let everyone know how my weekend went.

Arden's was easy, she only asked how it went. I responded that I would tell her on Friday, which is our standing happy hour group date. I'm going to bring Gavin. That should answer any lingering questions.

Ivy wanted some juicy details, so I texted her the selfie with Gavin's tongue in my ear, and told her she was right, no sex, but that I know all about his piercings now. I already know what she will say when she reads it. First, she is going to do a little internal squeal, then she is going to text back, *tell me, tell me, tell me.* Side note: I was wrong, she texted back, *tell me everything,* but I still know I was right about the squeal.

Miles will require more time, so I'll wait until I leave the office for lunch and then call him the old-fashioned way. My phone is still in my hand, and the dopy smile is still on my face when my boss pokes his head in my office.

"We need to talk."

"Right, *about that.*"

***

After a grueling morning and a very uncomfortable sit-down with my boss, I finally head out for a bite to eat at 2:45. I don't want to rock the boat any more than I already have, so I will keep it to thirty minutes. That will get Miles out of the way and maybe a muffin in my empty stomach.

He picks up right away, "Is it bad? It must be bad if you are calling me. What did you do? How could you have messed this up again so soon?"

"Number one, screw you for re-packing my bag."

"And two?" he asks with a smile in his voice that tells me he is already patting himself on the back.

"Number two, thanks for re-packing my bag."

"Cut to the chase. Is he any good in bed?"

"I wouldn't know, Miles, because he is a perfect gentleman."

"Horseshit."

"We didn't have sex."

"Liar."

"Well, not like sex-*sex*."

"I knew it. You tramp. Now spill."

***

When I leave the office at a respectable time of 5:05, instead of staying the few expected extra hours to catch up, I can feel my boss' glare on my back. It simmers just like the frown on his face. As he watches his golden child step on the elevator and out of his life for the evening, I can almost feel his blood pressure rising.

Look, I've been a model employee for damn near a decade. I deserve to leave at a reasonable hour *one time*. I was in my office with coffee in hand at 6:30 this morning. The problem with being the office workhorse is that all the extra work, all the *above and beyond*, all the *going the extra mile*—along with all the late nights and personal sacrifices, is that it becomes the *expectation*, not the excess.

Well, I'm over it. I recently decided to make some room in my life to care about more than my career and my Friday evening drinks with friends.

There. I'm happier already.

Now, I've got to get home and get ready for my date.

Chapter 27

My fingers tingle when I buzz Gavin up. I'm so excited to see him that I actually wonder if there is something wrong with me. I practically stepped over my mountain of work on my way out of the office—and I don't care. Normally, I wouldn't even sleep tonight because I would be fretting about everything left unfinished at work.

Now?

Now, I'm going to sleep like a baby.

Preferably after a couple rounds of insanely hot sex and sleeping like we're woven together—like we did in LA.

When Gavin walks in, the first thing I notice is his huge smile. The second thing is how sexy he looks all dressed up and polished. It's not until after a long lascivious kiss that I notice the flowers.

"You brought me flowers?" I ask, touched to the point of breathlessness. No one has ever given me flowers before. Well, I guess if you count the corsage Danny Eubanks gave me before junior prom, I've technically received flowers before. But had I known he would try and stick his skinny pecker in me all night, I would have just handed the corsage back to him.

"Of course, this is our first date," Gavin says, with no small amount of humor in his voice. He sets the lilies on the coffee table and adds, "I want it to be special."

I love that he considers this our first date, especially considering how many times we have been naked, or nearly naked together. Never mind how intimate our mouths have been with each other's bodies.

"I thought you said you don't kiss on a first date?"

"That only applies to bad first dates. This first date is going to be one for the record books," he says as he slides his hands up my thighs and underneath my dress. He discovers pretty quickly that I'm wearing a garter belt, and before I even know what's happening, he hoists me to his hips.

His kiss is smothering in the very best of ways. It gives the impression he missed me just as much as I've missed him. His hand roams to my essentially bare ass cheek, which precedes a deep, throaty groan.

"Are you trying to derail our first date, *Alabama?*" he asks as he squeezes my ass. I get the distinct impression he would smack it too, if it weren't our first date, that is.

"I made reservations at *Le Palais,* and I had to pull some strings because they are booked out for months. *Months*, Alabama. And then you go and put on sexy undergarments and almost make us miss our reservation." He slowly shakes his head in admonishment, but he has yet to put me down.

"You can think about my sexy undergarments while we savor our very special, first date dinner at the now *over*-booked Le Palais," I say as I squeeze my thighs around his body. The action provides just enough erotic pressure to realize it was a bad idea.

"I can *promise* you I will think about them at the restaurant—about how I will peel them off of you later." His words send a shiver through my body, except this shiver feels warm.

***

It took mere seconds to realize why people book Le Palais months in advance. I have never had a meal I would describe as exquisite—until now. Not that I could pronounce a single thing we ate, but each plated arrival was better than the last. And don't even get me started on the wine.

The company, however, puts the meal to shame. Gavin is sophisticated, he is funny, and he is completely charming. Right now, he looks like he is posing for a full-page cologne ad, and it is melting my panties right off. He's sexy on a bad day but put him in a suit, and he has enough swagger for ten guys. I would almost skip dessert to get him home sooner. *Almost.* We *are* at Le Palais, for heaven's sake.

"Alabama, show me your panties."

*record scratch

"Did you just—ask me to show you my panties?" My eyes must be literally bulging out of my head. I mean, we are drinking a $400 bottle of wine—in a chic and exclusive restaurant. Gavin even did the whole wine presentation ritual, with the swirling and the smelling. The panty request takes a quick sprint in the opposite direction.

Gavin pulls his phone out of the inside pocket of his suit coat, navigates to the video setting, and then maneuvers it into his lap and under the heavily starched table cloth. Oh my God, he is serious.

"I think the wine is getting to you," I tease, but if I'm honest, flashing my panties to his camera sounds kind of hot. Absolutely no one would suspect a thing because of the long table cloth—and, you know, the polished refinement of the restaurant.

"I think *you* are getting to me," he counters.

"I can't have something like that on your phone. What if you get mad at me and upload it to Instagram? Or worse, Pornhub?" Now, I giggle. Perhaps the wine is getting to *me*.

"Give me your phone then."

I think about it for a few seconds less than I should, and then fish my phone out of my purse and slide it across the table to him.

"You didn't unlock it."

"Seven seven zero one four."

The devilish look on his face should trouble me, but instead, it makes my heart rock heavily in my chest. While he swipes and eventually finds what he is looking for, I scoot forward, so my entire lap is concealed by the tablecloth.

Our waiter appears to pour the rest of our Pinot Noir and inquire if we would like another bottle. Gavin looks at me and with a raise of his eyebrows, asks if I would like another $400 bottle of wine. Um, no.

Once the waiter leaves, Gavin presses record and then slips my phone under the table, presumably to point it at my crossed knees. A second later, he sits forward and addresses me with steely focus.

"Your panties."

I gently pull my dress up my thighs until the bottom hem rests across my lap. Then I whisper to him, "I just pulled my dress all the way up, Gavin."

"Fantastic, now spread your legs for me."

I do, it feels dirty and sinful, but just the thought of exposing myself for him to video gets me excited. The G-string panties I have on are a laughable barrier, but I can still feel them impeding his eventual view.

"My legs are open for you, Gavin. Can you picture my thigh-high stockings and my garter belt?"

"Vividly."

"What about my bare skin above the stockings?"

"Yes."

"And the black satin panties between my legs?"

"Yeah, those have to go."

"Should I move them aside *and show you everything?*" I'm speaking so low, I can barely hear myself—but I'm not taking any chances with letting someone classy hear me sounding like a whore. However, speaking those words has me feeling like my spine could dissolve, and I wouldn't even notice.

"No, baby-doll, you need to take them off altogether and then hand them to me. But first, give me a little peak. Slide them to the side."

I don't break eye contact with him as I gather the scrap of satin and slowly pull it to the side. This is filthy, but it gives me a massive rush of endorphins. I even widen my legs more and really display myself for him. Thankfully, the video is on my phone.

"Can you picture it, Gavin? Nothing is in the way or blocking your view. You are taking a video of my exposed body *right now.*"

"This is hot as fuck, Alabama. Take your panties off and hand them to me."

This might get interesting. I made a point to put my panties on after the garter belt, so divesting myself of them will not be a problem, but handing them off sounds riskier than a prison yard drug transaction.

I don't possess enough stealth to remove my panties with any kind of finesse. Luckily, this is the moment our waiter arrives with the dessert menu. I would say he diverted Gavin's attention, but he didn't. Gavin didn't take his eyes off of me, not once. However, he did manage to order us a lemon tart, a vanilla bean crème brûlée, and a chocolate raspberry soufflé.

"Good choices," I affirm. I think it's cute he ordered three things. Having not discussed my preference in dessert, I think he wanted to be sure to get one I would like. As if there was any real danger of me not liking a dessert from a chic French restaurant. I wouldn't be surprised if the stuff in the trash tastes good here.

"I almost told him to bring us one of everything just to get rid of him, but I didn't want to get stuck here tasting them all," Gavin says with a good-natured laugh. I concur. I'm ready to be alone with this man.

Not one to skip a beat, he reaches across the table and extends his hand. I place my palm in his and smile before explaining that my panties are still around my ankles and that he needs to be a little more patient.

The hard part was covertly sliding them under my ass, the impossible part will be handing them to him. They will wad up fairly small, but I will still be passing my *underwear* across the table in an incredibly swanky restaurant. I'm more nervous about that part than I am about providing him with a Hustler shot commemorated on video.

"Before you hand them over, let me see what we've got so far. I'll start a new video when we are ready," he says just as calm as can be, as he withdraws the phone from his lap to view the footage. After a few seconds of watching his face suffuse with a self-indulgent grin, I can't take it anymore.

"Did it work? Or is it too dark? It's too dark, isn't it?" I nervously babble while praying no one walks by while he is sampling my immorality.

"I have the light on, it's perfect," he says as he deposits the phone in his jacket pocket.

As tiny as the G-string is, it is shocking how naked I feel without it on. After I pull one foot out of the panties, I cross my legs and cautiously lift my ankle to meet my extended hand.

Gavin looks dashing the way he relaxes back into his seat. He looks like he's at a high stakes gambling table in Vegas, and the look on his face says he knows he has the winning hand.

In an instance such as this, it's probably better to be quick than good. Still, I force myself to breathe deeply because this needs to be a smooth hand-off. When I wink at him, he leans slightly forward and opens his palm.

I ease my own hand forward and place it in his. Instead of taking the panties and withdrawing, he holds my hand casually for an insanely long time, considering what separates our palms.

"I want to thank you for coming to Los Angeles with me. Not only were you a big help, but you give incredible head."

When my mouth falls open, his quiet chuckle turns into a full-on laugh. A few heads turn but quickly grow bored and resume their pretentious conversations.

"No, seriously, though, I'm really enjoying getting to know why your friends paired us up."

"I am too. And, you're welcome," I can't say anymore because three delectable desserts have just been laid out before us. I can't even take my hand back in denial of what is held in our grasp because Gavin has yet to let go of me.

While the waiter busies himself arranging seven thousand spoons, Gavin effortlessly transfers my G-string into his jacket pocket. I wonder if the enticing desserts will distract him from my indecent display? He answers that by pulling the phone from his pocket and pressing record. Soon his hand is once again poised under the table and ready for action.

"Show me, Alabama. Open your legs for me." Apparently, I shift enough in my seat to convince him that my legs are wide open because he smiles brightly.

"They're open, *Gavin*," I taunt. They are, too, and the way I perch on the edge of the seat makes it that much more of a showcase.

"Touch yourself."

Here I hesitate for a few seconds because the exhibition is escalating rather quickly. However, the other restaurant patrons are completely oblivious to how badly we don't belong in here right now, and our waiter is busy at another table with the whole wine song and dance. So, I maneuver my hand under the tablecloth and touch myself.

I flutter my eyes closed to indicate very clearly to Gavin that my fingers have made contact. When I open them again, I can see his composure starting to slip.

"Slide two fingers up and down your slit, Alabama." I don't verbally respond, but I follow his directions while looking him square in the eyes.

"Are you wet?" he asks, without expelling any sound whatsoever. I give him my own wicked smile, and then I nod.

"Now, widen your fingers, and spread yourself for me."

I follow his instructions, but I also spare a thought to the thousand deaths I would die of embarrassment if anyone else were to see this video. I might have to burn my phone and switch carriers just to feel better. I'll have to nuke the cloud, too. I can't forget about the damn cloud.

"Damn, baby. You are making me so hard," he quietly groans. "Let's shovel this down and get out of here."

Chapter 28

Gavin's house is clean, but it's also kind of understated—like any dude's house before a woman comes in with paint, plants, and candles. His furniture is all nice, as are the lighting fixtures and wood floors. Notably, the white walls are all empty, which surprises me for the home of an artist. It just seems like something is missing. Maybe the heart, or perhaps the soul.

"I just moved in," he says, as he switches on a light in the kitchen and pulls open the refrigerator. That explains a lot, his art on the walls is just what this place needs. That would give it a heart *and* soul.

"I don't have much to offer you to drink. It looks like it's cold brew or water."

"I'll take water," I decide, though I'm not a single bit thirsty. When he hands me the glass of ice water, he also pulls me into a somewhat savage kiss, which rockets me to the place where I want to be naked and pressed up against his tattoos.

He must agree with that sentiment because he swoops me up like a newlywed and carries me to his bedroom. When he puts me down on his bed, he also takes away the glass of water. He puts it somewhere, who knows where, because now he backs me down on the comforter, and his kiss has not let up.

Besides his jacket, which he took off before we even got in the car, we are both fully dressed and panting like animals. While I fumble with the buttons of his shirt, he skims his hand up the back of my thigh to my ass, and then back down behind my knee to pull my leg up.

"I need to get to your zipper, or else this dress is going up over your head," he says as he rolls us to the side. Wasting no time, he unzips my dress and then unhooks my bra.

"Aww, this is an amazing bra, and you are going to miss seeing it," I tease. The way he has my knee pulled forward and cradling his body has my very naked core pressed up against his hard-on. It's all I can do not to grind myself against his designer slacks.

"I'm not going to miss a thing," he announces as he sheds his shirt and then works my dress down and off. I'm left in stockings, a garter, and a loosened black lace bra. He is all abs and smooth muscles—and his tattoos—I want them to brand me, mark me, I want them to imprint on my body, and claim me as his.

Gavin noticeably slows things down and reverts back to gentle, sweet kisses. When he touches my face and gazes into my eyes, I feel a soul deep connection with him I never could have anticipated. I didn't even see it coming.

My friends did, though. They deserve a Nobel Prize, too, because I didn't recognize the potential for us as a couple. I would have let him slip through my fingers. Just the thought of that makes me want to commit to therapy. Gavin and I fit—and this intense attraction is how galaxies form.

"You're beautiful, Alabama," he whispers, and it's so heartfelt and vulnerable that tears flood my eyes before his tenderness even fully registers. Guys have called me beautiful before, but never with such an ache—such a longing.

"Thank you," my voice cracks, and I blink a tear from my left eye, which Gavin swipes away with his thumb. I want to tell him that between the two of us, he is the beautiful one, but my throat clamps shut.

He doesn't seem to expect a loving declaration from me because he's already kissing me again—and slowly working his way down my neck.

Like I said, he can engage his tongue piercing at will. For the most part, when we kiss, I don't even feel the metal in his mouth—but times like this, when he intersperses little licks with his kissing, I feel the ball very deliberately. It's highly erotic, and I can't help but remember that same ball rubbing against other tender skin.

He works his mouth down between my breasts and then raises his head. His hair is tousled from my fingers, so he looks rugged and dangerously sexy while his hand skims over my stomach.

"You're right. This *is* an amazing bra," he says through a handsome grin. Then his palm slides from my belly, straight up and under the loosened lace to cup my breast and thumb my nipple.

"Too bad it has to go." Then his nose scoots the underwire over my other breast, and his mouth finds my nipple. I gasp at the intensity of the sensation, so he lifts his head and taunts, "You like that?" though there is little doubt that I do.

I pull him closer to me with the leg I have draped over his body, but it's not enough to relieve the pressure between my thighs. While his fingers toy with one nipple, his mouth works its magic on the other.

This is one of those instances where he capitalizes on his tongue piercing because he flicks and sucks my nipple like a pro, but when he bumps and rubs it with the ball of his piercing, he is a *master*.

"OhmyGod, Gavin," I pant as my back naturally arches against such skill. I'm starting to think he could bring me to orgasm without touching me otherwise.

He kisses his way across my cleavage and then switches breasts. Now, he is intently rubbing his tongue ring against my impossibly hard nipple. I seriously think he's going to make me come.

He alternates his intensity, and in this way, he rocks me closer to orgasm and then backs off some. I can't decide if I should hold on to him or grab handfuls of the blanket or one of each. I'm definitely going to— *Ughhhhhhhhhh!*"

Somewhere in the middle of the thunder crashing, his lips are on mine again. My kiss is half-hearted because there is so much happening down below, but his is perfect—and possessive. It's like he is taking back my orgasm and claiming it as his own. He should, he deserves it.

Eventually, our kiss evens out, but it's still a while before I can speak. I'm out of commission. My arms are even flopped down on the bed like I've been crucified. I have never climaxed from nipple play alone, and I need a few minutes to soak it all in.

"I need to taste you again before I'm inside you," he murmurs against my mouth. Life springs back into my arms, and I hold him tightly against me. I need to keep him in place. I do not want him to move a muscle.

"I don't think I can wait that long to feel you, Gavin." My voice comes out shaky, but I'm not surprised because my whole body is quaking with pure, animalistic need right now.

"No? You want my dick already?" he looks a little surprised, and a lot cocky. I can't believe I'm saying no to his sensational oral skills, but that would feel too distant right now. I need him pressed up against me, just like this.

"You sure you're ready?" he asks. Still a little inflated with his blue-ribbon abilities, and then needlessly reaches between my legs. "Mmmmm, you feel like you're begging for my cock." He swirls his fingers around my clit a few times and then adds, "Is that true, Alabama? *Are you begging for my cock?*"

I shouldn't have to dignify that with an answer because the evidence is all over his fingers, but if he wants to hear me say it, I'll say it.

"*Yeah, baby*. I'm so ready, I'm shaking from the thought of your cock inside me. I can't wait any longer. I need you so bad. *Pleeeease, Gavin*."

His fingers stop rubbing, but his hand remains between my legs, and he is looking at me with an unreadable expression on his face. A few more quiet seconds go by before he finally speaks.

"Well, that certainly was compelling, Alabama." Three seconds later, he springs into action and retrieves a condom from his nightstand. He is already unfastening his belt as he climbs back up on the bed. I sit up as he makes his way over to me on his knees.

"Let me," I say as I take over lowering his zipper and then push both his slacks and boxer-briefs down his thighs. Then he takes up the task and shoves them the rest of the way off his legs.

"Open the condom," I instruct before I take his swaying penis into my mouth. He doesn't need any help getting hard, but I want to provide some saliva to make sure the rubber slides for him a little.

After only a minute or two, he stills my head and slides out of my mouth. The condom is on in record time, then he pushes me back against the bed, knocks my legs apart with his knee, and then is on top of me. He doesn't go straight for the feather in his cap, but he does rock the underside of his dick back and forth through my folds. He kisses me passionately, too, so even though this is pretty fevered, it's still reverent and affectionate.

He has both of my wrists in one hand, pinning them above our heads, and he is kissing my neck when he enters me. He only pushes in part way, but the gasp that escapes my lips happens close enough to his ear to make him groan.

"God, I live for that gasp," he says as he drags himself almost all the way out. This time he pushes in further, and because we are kissing, my slow groan from being stretched open happens against his mouth. The feeling when he bores into me, with just the right amount of silky resistance, feels phenomenal with him.

Soon, his meticulous thrusts bottom out, and it feels so amazing I'm already sweating along my hairline. Now, each time he pumps, it's accompanied by a skilled hip roll that almost deposits my eyes in the back of my head. It's an advanced move—not all guys have it, trust me.

"Damn, girl—you feel crazy good against me," he grinds out. I can tell he is trying to restrain himself, but I'm not sure if it's for my benefit, or that he doesn't want to behave like a rutting bull. Perhaps he needs some encouragement—because I don't need him to be gentle with me.

"Harder, Gavin."

"I'm going to give you what you want, Alabama. In fact, I'm going to make you *crave* it."

Gavin does, in fact, fuck me harder, and now the neighbors are about to learn just how well he wields his cock. There is so much power behind his fucking. The harder he pounds into me, the more the tickle blooms inside my pelvis.

He slows the fury behind his stroke, but only so he can roll his hips and grind his pubic piercing into my clit. A splintered moan escapes my throat, but that's all the sound I make because I have to hold my breath against the mounting sensation.

Just as I start to feel the insistence of my approaching orgasm, he sits back, grabs my hips, and drags my shoulders down the bed as he keeps my body connected with his. Now my ass is completely off the bed as he changes our angle and gets to know my g-spot.

"*Gavin—*"

"*Oh my God—*"

"*Ahhhh—*"

"Have you got something to say, Alabama?" he teases.

"Just that—you're really good at this!"

"Aww, honey—I'm not even trying yet," he says with a smug little delivery. He might be telling the truth, though, because next, his thumb finds my clit, and it's all over for me.

Chapter 29

It's nearing midnight by the time Gavin parks in front of my loft. We debated me spending the night at his place, and he offered to bring me home early enough to wash all the sex off of me before work, but in the end, I decided it would be better to go home tonight.

He surprises me by turning off the car and taking his keys out of the ignition. The door to my building is twenty feet away, he doesn't need to walk me to the door. Then he turns to me with a serious look on his face.

"Alabama, I don't feel good about how that just went down."

"Wait. What? You don't feel good about it?" Now, I'm confused. A second ago, I thought he was going to walk me to the door like a gentleman. Now, he's telling me he has buyer's remorse?

"No, I don't," he pauses before going on, "I didn't want to fuck you senseless, Alabama. I didn't want to fuck you at all. I wanted to romance you. I wanted to be sweet and gentle with you, not behave like a rabid animal."

I don't respond right away, I just lean over and kiss him. He dropped a *grip* of cash on dinner tonight, and he still wanted to romance me. I'm not too sure I deserve this man.

"It's just not how I envisioned our first time together. I didn't want it to be all wild and unchecked like that," he explains.

"You want tender and romantic? Follow me upstairs."

"Are you serious?"

"Dead serious. Come on, I'll light some candles."

***

We are giggling like kids as we run up the three flights of stairs to my loft. Not because we are about to have sex again, but because I know damn well he is trying to smack my ass, and I'm only four steps ahead of him.

When we get to my door, he presses me against it for a pretty intense kiss considering we just ran up all those stairs.

"Listen to me, this is important," Gavin says. He is completely pressed against me, and he has only backed his face up far enough that our lips don't touch. Both of us are panting from the exertion, and even *this* feels sexy with him.

"I'm listening."

"You are going to have to curb your dirty talk for the night, ok?" he raises his eyebrows in question, and I burst out laughing. "I'm serious, Alabama. I can not be held responsible for what happens when your filthy mouth starts talking about filling you with my cock, or fucking your mouth, or any talk whatsoever of your pussy. Got it? I want this to be romantic and sweet."

"Ok, *Daddy.* Maybe you should bend me over your knee and spank me like the naughty little girl I am—"

"Jesus Christ, woman," he exclaims as he rests his forehead against mine. "What have I gotten myself into?"

"My panties, apparently. And next? Next is my bed."

***

Yes, Gavin is a rockstar at fucking, but he is equally good at romancing. The way he kissed me, and undressed me, and got all cuddly under the covers before licking me to another chart-topping orgasm, was pretty impressive. Maybe even legendary.

Now we are nestled together, kissing like we did that steamy night in Los Angeles. Like we can't get enough of each other. Except this time, my hand is on his dick, and I'm teasing his tip with his own pre-cum.

Ever mindful of his wishes for me to be a lady and not a whore, I don't mention anything about the head he is about to get. I just kiss my way down his ridiculous bod and moan with pleasure when I take him in my mouth.

The moan is for him, not me. I know he can feel all my vocalizations, so I lay it on pretty thick. There is nothing particularly awesome about giving blow jobs, but I love that I can dominate someone in this way. It is an incredibly powerful position to be in, and I get off on having so much control. I can reduce him to a puddle and absolutely destroy any fond memories of past blowies or past women. *That* is what a good blow job does. It provides him with a memory that sits front and center in his mind.

Mission accomplished. Gavin is grinding out the words, *so…fucking…good,* while wrenching his head back and fisting clumps of my sheets. When he shudders with near violent spurts of ejaculate, I paint his dick with it and let it all run down his shaft instead of swallowing it.

Again, as a lady, when I crawl back up his body, I do not tell him how much I liked sucking his dick or that I loved the taste of his cum. I just nuzzle my face into his neck and give him the sweet kisses he deserves. I mean, the guy was upset he didn't romance me enough before we had sex for the first time. Trust me, he is way too good for me.

I love when he holds or touches my face when he kisses me. It is so caring, and it speaks to our deep connection more than anything else. I know he will need some recovery time before round two, so I simply melt into him and revel in his talented lips and hands. I will sacrifice any amount of sleep to be with him, so I'm not in any hurry.

Before long, and without detaching our mouths, he rolls me to my back and enters me. His advance is agonizingly slow, but he presses all the way in. I have both hands on his neck and jaw, so I can't hold him in place and stop him when he starts easing out.

"Wait—" the word comes out almost frantic.

"Are you ok?" he asks, and I am, I just need a minute.

"Yes, I just—I just want to enjoy this feeling before you move again. You feel so, *so* good," I try to explain, but I can't do the sensation justice.

"You're shaking."

"It's because I'm so happy. You make me so fucking happy, Gavin," I admit. I'm a little surprised by my candor because I never get sentimental when it comes to sex, but this feels like so much more.

"You make me so happy too, *baby*. God, I want to live inside you. Wait. That didn't come out right. Those were two completely different thoughts strung together by great sex." We both laugh, him at his insinuation that he's only happy because he's balls deep at the moment, and me because of how horrified he is that it came out like that.

The humor sticks with us for a while, and every now and then one of us starts snickering at the memory. Which one hundred percent makes the other one start laughing too. It's cute—sweet, giggly sex. Almost cute enough to forget that Gavin isn't wearing a condom yet.

"What do you think of my pelvic piercing now that you've had a sample of it?" he asks on a backward glide.

"I think it should be a prerequisite for college. No! No, when guys get their driver's licenses. The DMV will be like, did you take defensive driving? Do you want to be an organ donor? Have you had the base of your dick pierced yet?" Now we are both howling with laughter, and it is maybe dampening the romantic vibe.

Gavin pulls out and then rolls to his back, "This might be a good time to suit up. Please tell me you have rubbers?"

I get off the bed and walk to the bathroom, where I keep them. It's not until I'm walking back to the bed, stark naked, that I realize none of my curtains are closed, and I'm parading around like I don't have cellulite.

Gavin is lying back against my pillows with both hands propped behind his head. His proud dick is still at full mast, so I give him an assist with the condom, and then saddle up. I'm not sure if cowgirl style sex is romantic enough, but as soon as his hands are on my tits, I no longer care about romance. Our laughing fits have already doused the sappy portion of our evening anyway.

***

When we finish, I collapse onto Gavin's chest, and he wraps his arms around me. We are fused together with sweat, and his penis is still inside me. I'm content to spend the rest of the night just like this.

"Stay with me."

"Of course, I'm going to stay with you. We just shared explosive sex, and I'm not really the high-five type of guy." He starts to get up, but I clamp my knees against his hips and keep him pinned beneath me.

"I'm just getting up to get rid of the condom. It defeats the purpose if millions of sperm still end up near your vagina," he says, and he punctuates his words with a sharp smack to my ass.

"Mmmmmm, that's so romantic, spank me again."

"Turn around so I can see your perfect ass, and I will," he says with conviction. I was teasing—because spanking someone doesn't usually rank super high in the romance department, but I'm a people pleaser, so I'll do what I must.

I turn around, reverse cowgirl, for the most part. Except that I lean forward and tip my ass up, giving him an *exceedingly* impolite view. Although, he doesn't seem to mind if his groan of *Ohhhhhh Yeahhhhhh*, is any indication.

He was serious about spanking me, though, because he swats me twice, spreading a prickling sensation that seems to encompass my entire lower half. It's not exactly the sharp slap I like, it's more the immediate aftermath—the receding tingle, and then the soothing palm.

Another smack, this one draws a moan out of me that I didn't expect. Then he rubs and squeezes my pink cheek before he does it again. This time, when he caresses my ass cheek, his other fingers don't remain idle. When I gasp, we both realize how sensitive I still am.

"We should get some rest anyway. I have a full schedule tomorrow—and you, *you* are going to land that big client, right?"

"How about we start with getting some rest?"

"Fair enough, now come give me a goodnight kiss."

Chapter 30

There is a strikingly transparent reason the work week is referred to as *a grind*. For me, that description is doubly so because I've yet to get caught up on sleep, and I can vividly feel the passion for my job slipping through my fingers.

I still work like a crazy woman while I'm here, but I'm less and less inclined to put in the long hours that once typified my day. The main reason being, I want my evenings back.

My boss seems to be getting used to the idea. Well, that might be a stretch, but he has been less purple and apoplectic the last few days when I've strut to the elevator to leave the office.

This week, being both a short week and my first week back from the tattoo convention, has been a gleaming example of how I've allowed various tasks to circle the shitter. First and very foremost is the big client I was expected to land an exclusivity agreement with. I wouldn't say my company is *out* of the running. I would just say I've led the charge in taking a quantum leap backward.

I've placated my boss with some impressive stall tactics, but eventually, I'll need to sign them or come up with a dazzling excuse for why I haven't. The problem is, it's damn hard to concentrate. Having Gavin on my mind while I'm at work is like running in concrete shoes— it can be done, but it won't be graceful.

Tonight, we are finally corking up the work week, and joining my friends for happy hour. Believe me, I'm just as curious as anyone about how it will play out. Arden and Brady will be there, and so will Ivy and the guy we picked out for her, Christian.

If that were it for the list of attendants, I wouldn't worry a bit because they all think the Gavin/Alabama set-up went off without a hitch. The wildcard of the evening will be Miles. And, although that designation is far from uncommon when it comes to him, I'm entirely right to be nervous.

Miles is the kind of guy that likes to start campfires with gasoline and a blowtorch, except that *that* whole scenario is just a metaphor for how he likes to conduct himself. Which is precisely why I consider him a wildcard.

***

The dreaded email came just before I left the office. My big client signed with another agency. It was a nasty blow, but not altogether unexpected. It also didn't stop my boss from trusting me with another coveted batch of promising accounts, which will percolate on my desk all weekend and then welcome me like a breath of fresh air on Monday morning.

Due to my bosses' thumb, of which I am still under, I leave work late and am the last to arrive for cocktails. While I make my way to the table, I notice a sort of dynamic equilibrium within the group, and since this is happy hour instead of physics class, I approach with caution.

Gavin absorbs me into his space with an arm around my shoulders and a just-short-of-chaste kiss to my lips. Evidently, he already penetrated my friendship circle like some sort of sexy osmosis and now looks like he was born into our group. Twenty minutes and enough charm for ten men, and he's already one of us.

The exception to the group is Christian, Ivy's date, who still looks a little uncomfortable. I immediately want to come to his aid because the pack of us is a lot to take all at once. We all acknowledge that simple fact.

"Christian, it's so good to see you ag—" I attempt.

"—**For** the first time *ever,*" Miles inserts. His execution is flawed, but it serves as a reminder that I have never, in fact, met Christian. I know a great deal about him, and think he is perfect for Ivy—but my familiarity with him is technically unwarranted.

Gavin knows the situation, but Christian most certainly does not. Ivy, in her perfect trustingness, allowed us to cherry-pick a boyfriend for her. However, like a star, she would collapse under her own weight if Christian were to find out about such deceit. Ivy would rather set her face on fire than be anything but honest and overflowing with integrity, so now I understand the ridged look on her face.

"Alabama, I'd like you to meet, Christian," Ivy adds like a tourniquet, and Brady signals the waitress for another round of drinks. He and Arden look like they are punching a clock and can't wait to get out of here to be alone.

For the first time, I understand the pull. It's been a consistent inside joke that the two of them always seem to have better things to do besides sitting around drinking with friends. Now, that same feeling sits on my lap like a weighty epiphany.

"Did you know they met on the same dating app we did? Isn't that an amazing coincidence and a testament to online dating in this day in age?" Gavin says with unnatural passion.

Miles has two choices here, skewer Gavin with a look that says shut-the-fuck-up, or jump on the bandwagon. He, of course, jumps on.

"Dating profiles make it so easy to choose someone almost *custom designed* for you, am I right?" Miles asks as he looks around the table.

"Yep, you just sit back and let the cream rise to the top," Gavin says, almost choking on his grin, as he looks directly into Miles' eyes. It's like they share a sarcastic brotherhood that bonds them together.

"Dating apps are great, but Arden and Brady's story is even better than that. He pulled her over and gave her a speeding ticket," I say, attempting to dilute the focus.

"That sounds like a story I need to hear," Christian says as he loops an arm around Ivy's waist and sweetly kisses her on the temple. That simple gesture swells my heart outside of the confines of my ribs.

"Why don't you stick to kissing your own kind?" a voice from behind us tosses out like a grenade. I stop breathing. Gavin tightens his grip on my thigh. Arden and Brady look at each other wide-eyed. Ivy's eyes fall to her untouched martini, and Christian's mouth drops open. In the same instant, Miles rises to his full height and, in two determined strides, stands toe to toe with a man whose friends have suddenly vacated their seats in favor of drinks at the bar.

"Looks like you are all alone in your ignorance," Miles grinds out. I have only seen him lose his temper a handful of times, and every instance has been in defense of someone else.

"Back off, man. I just think she needs to take up with someone more like her, that's all," the guy says as he tries to dismiss Miles and all his churning fury.

"If you mean someone who's devastatingly beautiful, or someone who possesses more kindness than you have in your entire family tree, or who is more intelligent and successful than you can ever hope to be, then yes, she should. The problem with little shit stains like you is that—much like your premature ejaculations, your ideas have no real value."

"I said back off, man."

This is the point where Gavin shifts his presence. I'm not sure whether he is getting ready to stop a fight or get a few blows in himself. I don't think he is even sure. Brady has also put some space between himself and Arden and watches the exchange intently.

"Sure, I'll back off just as soon as you apologize to my friends for having nothing but thin shit inside your brain." The guy starts to puff up his chest, but Miles leans in closer and stops the idiot from posturing.

The entire lounge area has taken an interest in the exchange, and not one single person will get in Miles' way. He is formidable when he is not angry, but the rage brewing right now makes him nearly lethal.

"And if I don't?" the guy questions, right before Christian steps up and spins his stupid head around with a well-placed fist.

"You had your chance, and that's more than you deserved," Christian says calmly. Miles is stunned but proud of Christian for the sudden change of events, and Gavin and Brady are already hauling the sack of shit away—presumably to introduce him to the cold, hard sidewalk.

Suddenly, the room is alive again. Christian extends his hand to Ivy, pulls her in for a kiss that makes the other three of us surprisingly uncomfortable, and then asks, "Are you ready for dinner, beautiful? I'll get us a table."

Chapter 31

Gavin and I are making a quick stop at his shop before heading back to his place for the duration of the night. I had fervently hoped he would forget all about the slutty video on my phone, but I had grossly underestimated his desire to watch the damn thing.

Once I weighed my own desires against the video, I decided I could get something in return. Which is why we are swinging by the tattoo shop. It took some convincing, but Gavin eventually agreed to show me a couple of the pictures he drew of me in his sketchbook.

Not all of them, mind you, he happens to be very possessive of his personal works of art. He finally agreed when I told him he could choose which ones to show me. It was I, who insisted he select one from the sexy batch of drawings, *and* one from the angry collection. I figure both will be incredibly insightful.

"I like how Christian handled himself tonight," Gavin says, breaking into my stream of thoughts. "I think it's important to have some balls as well as a softer side. You guys chose well for Ivy."

"I think so too. The hardest part about picking a guy for one of your best friends is that none of them seem good enough," I say as I meet Gavin's gaze. When he looks back at the road, I continue. "Well, in my case, I think my friends worried *I* wasn't good enough for *you*," I laugh, but there is truth behind my smile.

"Jury's still out on that, I suppose," he says as he takes one hand off the wheel and threads his fingers through mine—then starts laughing.

***

When we arrive, he locks the door behind us and leads me through the darkened shop to the open workspace in the back. Here he punches in a security code that will prevent the wail of sirens that normally follow the tripped alarm.

"You first," Gavin says. I think he is afraid I already deleted the videos. Had work not been so crazy, I might have. Sadly, I didn't think about it. I'm already burning with preemptive embarrassment as Gavin motions me into his tattoo room.

He presses a button that raises the back of his tattoo table, creating more of a recliner. Then, after toeing off his shoes and leaning back into his tattoo chair, he taps his thigh. Taking my cue, I sit on his lap and lean against his chest.

With nothing left to do except play the damn videos, I accept my fate and pull the first one up. The video is dark, and except for a few wild movements in the space between his hand and lap, it doesn't show any actual footage.

The second one is better, in that the space beneath the table is actually lit. You can see me raise my dress and then adjust the tablecloth before spreading my legs. The sexy part of the video is not even that my legs are open. It's the lace-topped stockings and the garter belt that really get your attention.

The sound is terrible, and we both sound like we are underwater but the outcome of the above-the-table conversation is me sliding two fingers underneath the crotch of my thong and then moving it to the side. There is a fair amount of shadow from my hand, so the open view is obscured a bit, but Gavin still has a visceral reaction to what we are looking at.

He slides his hand up the front of my skirt, and when the snug fit hampers his movement, he peels the restrictive clothing up my thighs.

He begins nibbling on my ear and, with warm breath, whispers into my sensitive ear canal, "Back it up a couple of minutes, and open your legs." I shiver just as much from the tickle in my ear as I do from the words he says.

When I widen my legs as much as I can while still keeping both of us on the chair, he follows along with the footage, slips fingers under my panties, and tugs them to the side.

When vacant air caresses my newly uncovered skin, I decide watching the video is a fantastic idea. I am boldly exposed to an empty room, but there is still a distinct thrill for me. Not only are we watching my shameless display on video, but the anticipation of his fingers touching me is nearly levitating me off the table.

The video jostles and then shuts off. While I ready the last one, Gavin wraps his fingers around the crotch of my panties and then roughly tugs them down my legs and off my body. Well, mostly off my body. He is unconcerned when they get hung up on one buckle of my way-too-sexy-for-work, strappy heels.

"The panties have to go, but the high heels stay. I'm looking forward to having those shoes in the air tonight." His words rumble in my ear and cause some incredibly vivid imagery to steal into my consciousness. The thought of being naked except for these shoes while we are together warms me from the inside. And that warmth is starting to bloom outward and become quite pervasive.

The last video starts off scandalous and then takes a rapid nosedive into downright depravity. It begins with my legs spread wide— no shadow or camera bobble to hide the showy boldness of my body. I instantly cringe, but when Gavin exhales, *Jesus, baby*, and runs his fingers over the live version, I have no further resistance to watching the video play out.

He mimics every timid motion I made beneath the table, and the effect lights me up like a rescue flare. Re-creating the action while watching it on the screen is far hotter than I ever could have guessed.

When he spreads his fingers, opening me up while watching the same rawness exposed simultaneously on the video, his shaky composure crashes to the ground and explodes into a million little pieces.

Before I can quantify his loss of composure, he slips two fingers inside of me and assertively gets to work. His control continues to slip as his need grows, and I can tell he is ready to make a run for home base.

"First, you are going to come all over my fingers. Then, I'll flash you two drawings from my sketchbook, as I promised. And then, I'm going to bend you over this tattoo chair and remind you how much I am your type."

As he rasps his fingers against my g-spot, he reaches up with his other hand and closes it around my neck. He isn't choking me, but his fingers restrict something because I can feel my pulse pounding in my swollen lips.

He releases my throat just as the first waves of orgasm break against the shore. However, he keeps moving his fingers until every last tremor has leached from my body.

"Say it, Alabama. Admit that, I'm your type."

"You are perfect for me, Gavin," I say, with no discernable resistance or any vocal inflection whatsoever. My body is wrung out, yet still snapping like a live wire.

He moves from behind me and retrieves his drawings from a locked cabinet. While I catch my breath, he flips quickly through the leather-bound book.

He wasn't kidding when he said he was going to flash them in front of me because he doesn't waste a moment letting me fully take them in. He shows me something very sexy and very naked, and then goes back to rifling through the pages.

"Gavin, I want to look at them. I want to see where your imagination goes. I want to know how you saw me back then." He lets out a heavy sigh and then joins me on the tattoo chair so that both of our legs are dangling over the side.

"Ok. This one was strictly based on your profile pictures. We hadn't really started to communicate beyond messages within the dating site. Actually, I should clarify that. I had only been exchanging messages with your friends at this point," he says as he cautiously hands over the book.

The page is open to the very sexy, very naked one I saw for a split second before.

"So, this was your fantasy version of me, right?" I ask as I study every pencil stroke.

"Sort of, I guess." He seems bashful of his work, or perhaps of his imagination. The drawing is a dead ringer of me—in the face and hair, that is. However, the spread-legged body is a different story. For one thing, the tits he drew, belong on a Playmate, and nobody's nipples stand out that far.

"This one is your orgasm face. I called that before we ever met," he says as he turns the page, granting me another forbidden look through his eyes. In the drawing, my head is thrown back in ecstasy while my fingers toy with my nipples. The top half of the drawing is full of life and detail. The bottom half is just a simple sketch of someone, presumably him, with his face between my legs. I think he is right about my o-face, though, at least that's what it feels like my face does.

"Gavin," I whisper, "You are insanely talented. If I could draw like this, my loft would be wallpapered with my art."

"You might be surprised. Drawing, much like journaling or poetry, is very soul-baring. It's harder than you think to expose yourself like that. Leaving oneself open to everyone's criticism will gut you in ways you never imagined."

"Who in their right mind would criticize this caliber of work?"

"The world is crawling with them, Alabama. And I can't afford to hang my worth on someone else's opinion. That's why the vast majority of my art will never see the light of day."

"I'm sorry you feel that way because you have more talent in your earlobes than most people could develop in a lifetime."

"I hope you still think that when I show you the next drawing," he smiles warmly, but his nervousness is evident.

"Please tell me I'm not hog-tied. Wait. I'm *not hog-tied,* am I?" I ask. He answers me by flipping through about twenty pages and handing back the open book.

"Nope, not hog-tied."

In the drawing, I'm in this exact room with my legs held wide open and my ankles tied to the base of the tattoo chair. My cheek is pinned against the leather, and my eyes are rolled back in orgasmic bliss. I am bent over and held down by a hand that has also wound itself in my hair to help restrain me. His other hand grips my wrists behind my back as he fucks me with what looks like a Coke-can-thick, monster penis. It also appears that cum drips thickly down my legs and pools on the floor beneath me.

Well, now. That wasn't so bad.

"That's a lot of cum, Gavin," is all I say, but I don't take my eyes off the image. It's clear in the drawing that Gavin is angry-fucking me, but I have to give him credit for portraying me as someone who enjoys that type of thing.

"Are you surprised? Look at the girth on me," he points out before taking the sketchbook back. After he locks it up, he shrugs out of his suspenders and starts unbuttoning his shirt.

"Enough about the drawings. I can't get my mind off those videos." He pulls me up from my seated position and lays a spine dissolving kiss on me while he finds my zipper, and works my skirt down.

After a somewhat clumsy few minutes of eager kissing and peeling off each other's clothes, we are both naked. I fully expect him to bend me over the table like he said he was going to earlier—and was graphically illustrated in his sketchbook. So, it surprises me when he again takes a seat on the hydraulic tattoo chair.

"Come here," he murmurs as he directs me to straddle his lap. The chair is versatile in that the back comes up, the foot part can drop down, the whole thing can lie flat—what it's not, is wide. In short, it's not exactly built for two, and there isn't much space for my knees.

"You better get a condom," I whisper between shallow kisses.

"Do you think I keep condoms at work? Alabama, I'm disappointed you think I fuck my clients," he is chuckling at the suggestion, but what he *isn't* doing—is worrying about not having a rubber.

"Should we stop then?" I ask, but the way I am stroking his hard-on conveys a different message.

"Of course not. What's the worst that could happen?" The way he is plucking at my nipples says he agrees with my hand and not with my objection.

"The worst? How about a baby or an STD—not necessarily in that order." Now he puts a palm on the back of my head and pulls me closer so he can nuzzle my neck.

"I don't have any STDs. Turns out, I'm a little more discerning about where I stick my penis than you give me credit for."

"What about a baby?"

"Are you telling me you are on *no* type of birth control?" he murmurs. His mouth against my neck, as well as his determination has not wavered a bit. His warm breath and tickling mouth are entirely unconcerned with such matters.

"What would you say if I said, I'm not on birth control?" I ask curiously.

"I'd say you were lying. Then I'd say we would make adorable babies." His certainty is well placed—about the birth control and the cute babies.

"I have an IUD," I admit.

"Then what are you waiting for?" he asks, as he drags me forward, up his lap, and skin to skin with his steel shaft. Our position forces my legs to stretch far apart, and leaves my knees hovering over the sides of the chair. Gavin grabs my ass and lifts me above his erection while I line it up and then slowly swallow him whole.

The narrowness of the chair doesn't allow for my knees to support my weight, or to properly raise and lower myself. Instead, I'm fully impaled.

The erotic feeling of fullness has paralyzed me from moving against him and made it hard to catch my breath. Gavin, more so than anyone else I've been with, requires me to take a few moments to adjust to the pervasiveness of his claim. His first thrust always seems to stop time for me.

Gavin finds my stillness and little gasps humorous, but at the same time, he isn't in the mood for any lengthy delays. With his hands still on my butt, he rolls my hips forward and back, rocking me against his body.

The sudden awareness of my sensitive skin grinding against his piercing takes me to a new place, and I begin to shamelessly gnash myself against the silver balls. My kiss becomes nothing more than a whimper that he answers with a chant. *Yeah, baby. Ride me. Just like that. Yessss, baaaby.*

Gavin pulls me tightly against his body and holds me there. I don't know if it's to slow me down, or to help smash his piercing into the volatile bead of my clitoris, but if we keep up this desperate grind, I'm going to come way too soon. I can't stop, though, it's impossible for me to stop.

I feel like I'm about to come unglued, and have some sort of spiritual experience. The combination of his bare cock buried inside me and the torment of the metal balls is borderline too much. I've gotten here too quickly. I'm chasing oblivion, and there is no hope of him catching up.

"Gavin. It's too much. I can't—"

"Let go, baby. I'm right there too," he coos against the little indented hollow of my throat. "I'll follow you."

When I climax, it's throaty and unrestrained. When he follows a moment later, he squeezes me tightly against his body and shivers with each guttural surge of his pulsing orgasm.

Our recovery is lengthy, considering how quickly we both came. I think the feel of bare skin instead of filmy latex played a big role, but also the videos and his drawings. I've never had sex in a hydraulic chair before, but it was insanely good the way the position pitched me forward on his lap and against his piercing.

"Are you going to delete the videos?" he asks, somewhat out of nowhere.

"Yes. One hundred percent," I say definitively. He will never be able to convince me not to. He seems fine with my declaration as he sits forward while also laying me back on the table. Now his legs dangle off the sides while I'm spread open and splayed out before him.

"I want to see something before you delete them," he says as he drags his thumb around my semen-soaked vagina. My position makes his view rather raunchy, but him dallying with his own cum is downright filthy. I don't ask what he means, but I smile knowingly because I assume he wants to see them again.

"I want to watch my cum ooze out of your body. Then you can delete them." He punctuates his statement by sinking his thumb inside me and then watching with primitive, lust-soaked eyes as the displaced semen dribbles out.

***

Once we get back to his house, it's after 10:30. We are both so exhausted, we abandon the attempt at watching a movie in favor of brushing our teeth and falling into bed.

As good as our sex is, this is what I crave from him. The intimacy of being held like this—kissed like this. It feels right. It's effortless in a way that needs no convincing. We fit together—in very simplistic terms, and also in incredibly complex ways that continue to baffle me.

"How did work go this week? There has been so much going on since we got back, we haven't had a chance to discuss that huge account. I will feel so guilty if you lose it because of me," he says as he strokes the hair away from my cheek with his thumb. I love that even naked and in bed, he still wants to dial into other aspects of my life. It adds to the feeling of this being universally right.

"First of all, you have no reason to feel guilty. You had no part of any of that. Second of all, they chose to go with a competitor. But, more importantly, you should know that I have no regrets. I would do the same thing a hundred times over if faced with the same choice."

"Oh, damn."

"Gavin, had I not gambled that account, I wouldn't be here with you."

"Then, I'm glad you did. I'm just sorry you had to."

"I'm not. I could have twenty of those accounts and still feel something missing. However bumpy the path was, I'm glad it led me to you. I wouldn't change a thing."

"You wouldn't change our first date?" he grins with the question.

"I don't think so, it was kinda fun earning your attention. Plus, you said you don't kiss on the first date," I say as I palm the back of his neck and pull him in for a kiss.

"You also said, I wasn't your type either," I point out mid-kiss. He backs his head up and looks me directly in the eyes.

"Let me be very clear about something," he says with some discipline behind his words. "*You* are exactly my type." Then his mouth is on mine again before I can share the sentiment.

Whenever I think about how close I came to pushing him away, my throat tightens reflexively. Looking back, it's absurd to me that I almost missed it. At the time, the voice inside my head that may have whispered, *give him a shot—you might be surprised,* was overwhelmed by something else. Something self-sabotaging. Something that filled in all the blanks for me, instead of letting fate do it naturally.

Gavin takes a break from our kiss and lays his cheek against his bicep. I turn to face him, my own cheek against the pillow. Our faces are inches apart, but our arms and legs still entwine together. Our bodies feel symbolic of our union, and this is a moment I will remember forever.

We are meant to be together. I know that now with crystal clarity. My friends knew it all along. Me? I just had to learn to trust the process and believe in the path I was on.

KC Decker

Epilogue

Friday evening happy hour, one year later…

Ivy is already showing, and at just over four months along, she is becoming more and more uncomfortable at our twice-monthly happy hours. Not that she is physically uncomfortable because that chick is nothing but poised, and would be graceful with two broken legs—but she tends to get some funny looks as she sips her virgin cocktails.

Christian is ecstatic about being a father and could not get a ring on her finger fast enough. The two of them were perfectly designed for one another—Just ask Miles or Arden, or better yet, ask me—I was the one that pushed for Christian when Miles and Arden were torn between two possibilities.

Arden and Brady have itchy feet, so they spend as much time as possible globetrotting the world. They decided a long time ago to get all the traveling out of their system before they tie the knot. Their reasoning is because, for some reason, they believe marriage equates to insta-babies.

Though they were not cherry-picked for each other by meddling friends, they are a good example of fate intervening to bring two people together. I mean, come on—a cop and a speeding ticket? Isn't there a whole genre of porn based on that very thing?

Miles is, of course, here too. Now, he is a different breed altogether because he never, ever wanted to settle down with one person like the rest of us. However, I will say that he has started bringing Everett around more and more, and I recognize a certain glint in Miles' eye when it comes to him.

He may fight it every step of the way, but he is falling in love. Soon enough, that crazy emotion will grab on like a Kraken and pull him under, so he can drown in the sappiness like the rest of us.

Phillip and Sunrise are in town for a few days too. They certainly infuse a little spice into the group, and it does my heart good to see them together. They are not just together, together—They went into business with each other as well.

As far as Gavin and I, we will spend weeks at a time at my place or his, it makes no difference to either of us as long as we are together. Both of us are in the same headspace about work too. We are at the top of our game career-wise, but that intense drive that used to push us to be the best is starting to falter more and more. Simply put, our jobs have taken up residence in the back seat.

Things between us are still smoking hot. Though, at times his artistic requests will terrify me a little. Not that they are scary in the literal sense. More like, scary in the sense that one day our kids or grandkids may come across some of his drawings. He is an artist, and I am most definitely his muse.

One such artistic session happened after Ivy and Christian's Roarin' 20's engagement party. Ivy, Arden, and I all had professionals do our hair and makeup, so we looked like we just stepped onto a Hollywood set for a scene from The Great Gatsby. I wore a sexy, beaded chiffon dress, a glamorous vintage 20's headband, and layers upon layers of pearls. Hands down, best night of my life.

Well, when we got back to Gavin's, he wasn't satisfied with the hundreds of photos we must have taken throughout the night—So, he stripped me naked, except for the pearls and vintage headpiece, and then posed me in the most provocative manner he possibly could. After that, he captured the whole thing on a four-foot by six-foot giant canvas.

"Alabama, what's that dopy smile all about? Are you high?" Miles asks from across the table. Because our group is so big, almost everyone is engaged in smaller conversations, so only Everett, Gavin, and myself hear him.

"I guess I'm just feeling nostalgic, that's all," I smile wistfully. I think it unnerves Miles that I don't shoot something snarky back, but this exact bar at this designated happy hour is where it all started.

"Well, knock it off," he says as he leans back to where Everett has his arm draped over the back of Miles' chair.

"Don't worry about him, he's just chapped that he lost a bet," Everett explains as he tightens his arm around Miles' shoulder. Then he flashes a huge smile that Miles can't help but return. Yep, there it is. The glint in his eye.

"What was the bet?" Gavin asks before raising his beer bottle to his lips and taking a sip. His other arm is casually over the back of my chair as well.

"Miles here didn't think we would last a month. He said I wasn't his type."

***

Gavin left his phone at work, so on the way back to his place, we had to make a small detour. Every time we come to the shop after hours, I feel like someone is going to see us moving around inside and call the police. The reception area at the front remains lit, but everything else is closed up and shut down. So, even though we have every right to be here, I always feel a little like I'm breaking the law and am about to have a gun drawn on me.

I follow him into his tattoo room, where he flicks on the light and walks straight across the room for his phone. I freeze in the doorway because prominently hung on the wall is a gigantic drawing of me. It's done in the same style as the Buddha in the piercing room, so it looks like I'm alive and about to step down from the wall and go about my business.

It's also the one Gavin did after Ivy and Christian's party, but different. I look glamorous, and shockingly sexy draped only in pearls. Thankfully, he left out the vulgar part with my legs open.

Anyone else could look at it, and the first thing they would see is all that red hair, or maybe my eyes, possibly even the side-boob with pearls covering my nipple—but me? I see something else right away.

I see the one glaring difference in the piece—I see the little detail that differs from the night Gavin sketched it. In the drawing, my left hand is still posed sensually against my face, but now Gavin has drawn a diamond ring on my wedding finger. Suddenly, all I can hear is the woosh woosh woosh of blood circulating between my ears.

"Gavin," I whisper. I must look like I've been lit up like an angel because that's how I feel. "What is that?" I ask. I know it's me, there is no question it's me. What I'm asking about is the ring.

"Oh, that?" he points over his shoulder with his thumb, as if it's no big deal—just another perfectly rendered portrait hanging in his shop.

"That's my future wife."

Also by KC Decker:

Standalone Books

Little Dove

My name is Etta Freeman.

There is something special about me.

Not special in a good way, though, more like special in a way that will get me killed one day.

It's not something I talk about with anyone, but that doesn't stop me from trying to snare my neighbor in my devious web.

He is angsty and brooding and completely sexy in a scrappy, bloody knuckle kind of way.

I should also mention that he's a scheming, felonious drug dealer and I'm drawn to him like flies on shit.

The problem is, he doesn't yet know his role in my narrative, but he will fall in line.

They always do.

Trigger Warning: Little Dove contains content that some readers may find distressing.

Of Ash and Angels

* Silver Medal Winner of the International Reader's Favorite Book Awards

Justin:

I've never had a therapist I didn't want to punch in the face. As a collective group, they all say there is no way around grief, only through it, but for me, grief has become who I am. The idea of shedding it is as ludicrous as stepping outside of my own skin.

The fact is, some things can break you. I mean, shatter your soul and cast it into the wind in a billion tiny pieces. To think you might one day be able to find all those infinite pieces of yourself, patch everything back together, and move on with life—well, I don't even need to dignify that with a response.

Norah:

A few months ago, I shaved off a hundred and eighty-five-pound parasite. Then, once I was rid of him, I wondered why I didn't stick it out because the dating world is treacherous these days. Turns out, so is unemployment.

I suppose, to offset all the swiping left and streaming marathons in my life, I should take this job. There is a massive problem with the position, though.

The problem's name is Justin Abernathy.

Gradation

Friends. Ride or die, right?
Always have your back.
Know all your dirty little secrets.
Love the shiny parts of you, and embrace the crappy ones.
Yeah? Well, I don't know about all that nonsense because my friends are a bunch of assholes.
They're taking over.
They're commandeering my love life.
They're constructing a dating profile for me, and it's bad...
Because I don't even have the *password* for it,

and I have to do *exactly* what they say.

Mercy

**INTERNATIONAL BOOK AWARDS FINALIST and
KIRKUS FEATURED REVIEW RECIPIENT!**

My parents abandoned me a decade ago to the walls of this
institution. They believed my troubled childhood mind was
something sinister instead of homegrown or explainable. The
truth is that my condition is complicated. It's messy and often
misunderstood.

I've worn all types of labels over the years: Non-believer, pariah,
deranged, *orphan*... It's all in my file if you care to understand
me better. However, the label that implanted the deepest and
garnered the most attention is the one I wear, like a Scarlet
Letter. It precedes me when I enter a room and gets whispered
about like a schoolyard crush.

Paranoid Schizophrenic.

Dr. Sutton has some lofty ideas about my condition and claims
mental illness is only one aspect of hundreds that make me who I
am. Not one to shy away from a challenge, he thinks he can help
me. His confidence is legendary, but I've carried this burden for
a long time. Despite what he thinks, I can't be fixed.

He doesn't realize I'm falling for him or that I have some lofty
ideas of my own. He should know better because people like me
deserve a hero, too.

The Jessie Hayes 4 Book Series
(Must be Read in Order)

1462 South Broadway (Book 1)
Winner of the National Excellence
in Romance Fiction Award)

It's said that a bird never has to doubt the stability of her branch because her trust is in her own wings.

I myself, am trying to grow some wings of my own, but I'm kind of mired in place right now.

My roommate fondly calls my situation *a rut* and seems to think he knows how I can climb out of it.

The problem with his solution is that he's stone-cold crazy.

There is no way in hell I'm going to a *sex club*.

A scorching, witty, and unexpectedly tender story about finding courage in the unlikeliest places—and discovering the kind of freedom that doesn't come from a stable branch, but from daring to fly.

720 Linden Street (Book 2)

My kinky introduction to BDSM has been less about dipping my toe and more about being tossed into the deep end…bound.

That simple fact has required me to make some pretty hefty leaps outside of my comfort zone.

Turns out, there is a whole lot more to the BDSM scene than I initially thought.
There's a staggering array of possibilities, all wide open for me to see and experience.

You see, my boyfriend owns a sex club.

And I have a lot to learn.

Trigger Warning: 720 Linden Street contains content that some readers may find distressing.

1700 Grant Street (Book 3)

Have you ever found yourself at a crossroads on your journey, with your entire future depending on tiny little decisions here and there?

Do you resist temptation and stick with your current choice? Or will you always wonder how life *could have been*?

When you get to this branching of your life's path, it's not enough to merely choose one direction. You must distance yourself from the rejected road. Because dancing between the two will slowly unravel you.

And it will start with your fickle heart.

945 Cedar Avenue (Book 4, Salinger's Story)

A wedding engagement is a joyous occasion, right?

Well, I suppose that depends on your perspective.

If you happen to be on the side of the path that branches to the left, when the love of your life chooses to go right, you may have a different opinion.

So, what do you do when someone else's choice annihilates the future you counted on?

The answer to that may depend on your membership status at a certain sex club.

Namely, 1462 South Broadway.

COMING SOON!

The Space Between

Midnight Sun

JOIN KC DECKER:

Mailing List: www.KCDeckerBooks.com

Instagram: www.instagram.com/author_kc_decker

X: www.X.com/KCDeckerBooks

Facebook: www.facebook.com/kc.decker.79

Bookbub: www.bookbub.com/profile/kc-decker

www.KCDeckerBooks.com

Acknowledgments:

One day, I'd like to use this space to thank the team of professionals working tirelessly behind the scenes with me. I'd love to acknowledge the industrious agent, the meticulous editors, and the mighty publishing house whose support is critical to my success. But today is not that day because I don't know any of those people. So I'm free to thank the real heroes who deserve my gratitude. The late-night readers. The book-clubbers. The just-one-more-chapter fanatics. The bleary-eyed sleep-sacrificers. The paperback traditionalists and ebook devotees. It's readers whose unabiding faithfulness deserves my recognition. Whether through page reads, reviews, word of mouth, or blog posts, your support means everything to me. You are the ones who deserve my thanks because, without all of you, there is no me.